COP
JAGGED EDGE
SERIES #2

By A.L. Long

Cop: Jagged Edge Series #2

Interior edited by H. Elaine Roughton
Cover design by Lucas Schmauser
ASIN: B01HMRX1CM
ISBN: 978-1533465849

This book is intended for mature adults only

Acknowledgment

To my husband of many wonderful years, who has been so supportive of my writing. If it weren't for him my dream of writing would have never been fulfilled. I love you, sweetheart. And to my family, whom I also love dearly. Through their love and support, I can continue my passion for writing.

To the many readers, who took a chance on me and purchased my books. I hope that I can continue to fill your hearts with the passion I have grown to love.

A special thanks to all of the people that supported me at SPS. If you would like to learn about what they can offer you to become a self-publisher, please check out the link below. You will be thankful you did. https://xe172.isrefer.com/go/curcust/allongbooks

Table of Contents

CHAPTER ONE

Sabrina

So it doesn't matter how hard I try, I just can't get my legs to cooperate with the rest of my body. Maybe it is due to the insecurities that I have had to deal with most of my life or maybe it is the fact that a hunky piece of man candy is standing before me with only a pair of shorts hanging low on his hip. There should be a law against a man showing such a gorgeous body, knocking every woman off her feet.

"If you don't concentrate on your center, Brie,

you are going to end up getting the shit kicked out of you," Tyler said, releasing me from my naughty thoughts.

"Yeah, yeah, whatever. That's easy for you to say. Can't you put on a shirt or something?"

Once Tyler grabs his shirt, I'm finally able to concentrate on the task at hand. Tyler is the self-defense trainer that was assigned to me when I signed up for the course. I was tired of being defenseless against a man. I was tired of being used as a punching bag as well. My ex, Sean Bishop, will never lay another finger on me. Even with the restraining order I had placed on him, he still managed to get to me. I needed to be prepared. So when I heard about a class they were offering for women at the YMCA, I jumped right on joining. What was even nicer was the fact that it was free.

"Okay, one more time, Brie. Concentrate on your center," Tyler said, taking his stance behind me while wrapping his arm around my neck from behind. Tyler has at least one hundred pounds on me, so for me to be able to flip him over my shoulder is nearly impossible. Finding my center, I bend my left leg and step back enough to give me the leverage I needed to pull his weight over my shoulder. Closing my eyes and giving it everything I had, I concentrated hard and prayed that I didn't end up hurting myself in the end. Opening one eye and then the other, his body was lying flat on the mat.

"I did it! Oh my God!" I jumped for joy and did a victory dance around Tyler's body. When he rose to a sitting position, I could tell he was not one bit amused by my celebration.

Pushing himself to his feet, he said with annoyance, "Are you going to dance around all day or are you going to focus on learning what you came here to learn?"

Being flipped must have hurt his ego because he wasn't so easy on me the rest of the lesson. By the time I got back to my apartment, my body felt like it had been through the wringer. I didn't think there was a muscle in my body that didn't hurt. Matter of fact, I think muscles that I didn't even know I had were sore.

Throwing my things on the couch, I walked to the fridge and grabbed a bottle of water before I headed to the bathroom for a much-needed soak. I was glad that it was Friday because I knew it would take that long for me to recoup from my defense class. While the tub filled with water, I slowly removed my clothes. Looking in the mirror, I pulled my hair back into a loose bun. Even though I had a fit and toned body, one imperfection was always there right in front of me. It was something that stared back at me every day. Over time it had gotten lighter, but it was still there. The scar stretching from my navel to the right side of my body just above my hip was a reminder of how close I was to losing my life.

Sliding in the tub, I leaned my head back against the spongy bath pillow I bought at one of those bed and bath stores. It was the best investment I had ever made. Another investment I didn't regret was the Taser that I never went anywhere without. It had been my security blanket for the past seven years. I don't know what it was, but I always managed to attract the wrong kind of guys. It was that way seven years ago and it's that way now. At least I was smart enough to break if off with my now ex Sean before I ended up in the morgue. Even though he had only hit me one time, it was one time too many. I was never going to let another man ever hurt me again.

Pulling myself from the lukewarm water, I lifted the lever on the tub and let the water slowly drain out. Once I was dried off, I pulled the miracle ointment from my medicine cabinet and began applying it to the scar. It became a daily ritual for me to apply the ointment once in the morning and once at night. The nurse at the hospital I was taken to, said it would help reduce the signs of the scar. She must have known how ashamed I was of it and how ugly it was. In my eyes it was even uglier than the way I had gotten it, only because I knew how it came to be. That was the day my life changed forever.

Removing the hair tie from my hair, I headed to my bed for some much-needed sleep. Gathering my thoughts, I couldn't help but wonder what it would feel like to be with someone who actually cared about me. It was something that I had always wanted: to be loved by someone as much as I loved them. I guess I could always dream. I knew that my chances of finding such a person were next to nil. I had a better chance of getting struck by lightning than ever finding love.

~****~

The next morning, I could hear the birds singing outside my bedroom window as I laid in bed thinking about my life. It was just the beginning of summer and everything was in full bloom, and everything should be cheery and happy. The only problem was that was not the case, at least with me. Yes, I had a wonderful job that I loved and Lilly Davis was the best boss ever. I should be happy, but the one thing I needed more than anything was missing, to have someone love me.

Finished with my pity party, I rose from my bed and decided to make something special of this glorious day. After taking a quick shower, I decided to stop by the Happy Cow and say 'Hi' to my ex co-workers.

When Lilly offered me the job to be her assistant at Séduire Art Galley, I never thought I would enjoy working there as much as I did. I decided to put in my notice at the Happy Cow and focus my time on being the best assistant ever to Lilly. It was hard saying good-bye to all the people I worked with, who were also the only family I really had. The one benefit of working at the gallery was that the Happy Cow was right across the street so it was almost like I never left.

I would have loved to spend time with Lilly, but I knew that she and Peter were still on vacation in the Bahamas for a week. I told Lilly that I thought Peter was going to pop the question, but Lilly thought I was out of my mind. I will know whether or not I was right in a couple of days.

After Lilly moved out of her condo to live with Peter, I didn't see the hunk of everything that is man standing in front of her door. Except when he used to come around the gallery, at least until he got called away on some important mission. I wasn't sure where he went, but I hadn't seen him around in about a month. It must have been pretty important to take him away for so long. He seemed really nice, someone I wouldn't mind getting to know, even though I felt like I really wasn't his type. Not by his caliber of feminine characteristics anyway.

As I headed out the door, I heard a strange noise behind me. Looking over my shoulder, I saw an overweight Siamese cat scratching at the door. I wasn't sure what was going on, but I knew that Mrs. Jensen would never let Oliver out of her condo. Walking over to him, I picked him up and knocked on her door. When she didn't answer, I began to worry.

Knocking a little harder, I said, "Mrs Jensen, it's Sabrina from down the hall. I have Oliver. He must have got out. Mrs. Jensen, are you at home?"

There was still no answer. What if something bad happened to her? Walking back to my apartment with Oliver, I decided to call 9-1-1 to see if they could make a courtesy visit. I wasn't sure if it was a real emergency, but the dispatcher said she would send a unit right over.

While I waited for someone to come, I treated Oliver to a bowl of milk. I wasn't sure how long he was perched in front of her door, but he seemed to enjoy the warm milk. I never could understand the life of a cat. What a life. Oliver seemed to be content wherever he was. After he finished his milk he jumped on the built-in sitting area below my living room window and began licking himself clean. I guess he was enjoying the heat that the sun was radiating through the window.

Only ten minutes had passed before a response team knocked on my door. Leaving Oliver in the comforting sun, I walked with the two male responders to Mrs. Jensen's condo. When they were unable to get an answer on the other side of the door, one of the men turned around and kicked the door open right below the doorknob. *"That is going to hurt Mrs Jensen's wallet,"* I thought to myself, knowing she was on a fixed income.

As the responders walked into her condo, I followed behind. It wasn't until I saw her lying lifeless on the kitchen floor in a puddle of water that I began to panic. I wasn't sure what happened to her. I only hoped it wasn't anything serious, but when she didn't respond to their voices, I knew it was bad. The EMT guys began checking for vitals, but it was no use. She didn't have a pulse, and based on the coldness of her body, she had been lying there for some time. One of the men looked at his watch and said, "I'm calling it. I'll let dispatch know to send a unit by."

Even though I didn't know Mrs. Jensen very well, she was a sweet old lady. I remember her inviting me over for a cup of tea and biscuits. I could listen to her for hours the way she talked about her childhood in London. I just loved the way she talked. Now she was gone. I wasn't even sure if she had any children. I never did see anyone stop by to visit her. It was sad that she didn't have anyone.

The police showed up a short time later and I gave my statement, letting them know what had happened. They offered to take Oliver off my hands and to a pet shelter, but I refused to let them take him. I knew exactly what could happen to a cat his age. I loved animals, but really never had the time for them. I guess acquiring a new pet would change that.

Finishing up with the police, I walked back to my condo. When I opened the door, Oliver was still in the same spot that I left him in. Walking over to him, I picked him up and gave him some love. Holding him up so that he was looking at me, I said softly, "Well, Oliver, it looks like you are going to have a new home. Sorry, but your mommy died, but it will be okay. I'll take care of you." Somehow I had a feeling he understood every word I said. Either that, or he sensed that I had lost my mom too.

CHAPTER TWO
Sabrina

"God, I'm too young to start getting hot spells," I said out loud, my body overheating. Throwing the covers off of me, I realized that it wasn't my body overheating, it was the white and gray fur ball that was nestled against my lower stomach and my hip. Nudging Oliver, I tried everything I could to get him to move. At least I knew that he was still alive, by the way he was purring and digging his claws into my mattress. Giving up all hope of sleeping in, I pushed away from my new roommate and headed to the bathroom. Looking in the mirror, I grabbed my toothbrush while I waited for the water in the shower to warm up. Stripping off my ratty pajamas, I stepped inside the shower and soaked up the hot spray.

As I got ready for the day, I thought about all the things that I needed to do. With Oliver as my new roomy, the first thing I absolutely needed to do was buy him some treats and cat food. I hated the fact that I didn't have a car and needed to to take the subway or walk nearly two miles to the nearest pet store and market. Grabbing my purse, I decided to endure the walk to the pet store and take the subway on the way back. This way I would be able to kill two birds with one stone. I could get in my morning workout and save money on the subway fare.

When I got to the pet store, I couldn't believe the variety of pet food they had. I wish I knew what kind of food Mrs Jensen fed Oliver, it would certainly make my life a lot easier. Picking the midrange priced food for adult cats who were overweight, I place the 20 pound bag in my cart, along with some other items, and proceeded to the checkout.

After paying fifty bucks at the pet store and then another thirty at the market, my wallet was bare except for my I.D. and credit card that already reached its purchasing limit. Even though Lilly paid me well at the gallery, it barely covered my monthly house payment and other essential expenses. It was for this reason that I needed to find a new place to live. That and the fact that my ex found out where I lived.

Setting my bags on the counter, I grabbed the bag of cat food and the food and water bowl that I purchased for Oliver, and began filling one bowl with a small amount of food and the other with cold water. Calling for him, I waited as he slowly moved down the hallway in my direction. Once he spotted the food, his pace picked up. I thought it would be best to purchase him a litter box and litter as well. Filling the box with just the right amount of litter, I headed to the bathroom where I placed his box in the corner, out of the way. Hopefully he would figure out where his new box was instead of using the makeshift cardboard box I had stuffed with shredded magazines.

After I put everything away, I took a seat in my favorite spot and booted up my laptop. If I was going to have a chance at saving money, I needed to find a new place to live. There were a lot of apartments to rent. Unfortunately, they were all out of my price range unless I wanted to live on the lower Eastside of Manhattan. The only other option was to see if anyone was looking for a roommate. Changing my search, I waited as the wheel began to spin. My search brought up several possibilities. One was a student looking for someone to share the rent for a two-bedroom apartment near Central Park on Columbus. The only problem was they didn't accept pets.

Getting discouraged, I decided to put my search on hold and visit my friends at the Happy Cow. Oliver seemed pretty content where he was, so I grabbed my things and headed out the door. Hailing a cab, I headed to the Happy Cow. When I arrived at the small coffee shop, the people I used to work for came at me in a swarm. I guess they really missed me. I've missed them, too. Even though it had only been a couple of months since my departure and I came by almost every day that I worked at the gallery, they acted like they hadn't seen me in years.

Propping my elbows on the counter I order a small Mocha Latte. Everyone who greeted me went back to what they were doing. I took a seat at one of the high tables against the window and watched the people as they walked by. I was so focused on them, that I didn't hear Nikki coming up to me with my Mocha.

"Here's your Mocha, Brie," she said, placing it on the small table. "This one is on me."

"Thanks," I said, grabbing the warm cup and taking a sip.

I watched as Nikki walked away. She was one of the better coffee servers. She was also the best at making Mocha Lattes. She was always applying for modeling jobs. It surprised me that Cover Girl hadn't swept her up. She was beautiful in a wholesome kind of way, almost like she was raised on a farm or out in the country. She never wore too much make-up and her skin was absolutely flawless, something I think every girl wished they had.

"Hey," she said, turning her position as she looked at me. "If you want, I can give you a ride when I get off. I should be done in about thirty minutes."

"That would be great," I replied, grateful that she offered.

Nikki and I had become pretty close while we worked together. She told me things about her life that she didn't want anyone else to know. Even though my life was a shit storm compared to hers, I felt her pain nonetheless. After all, who in their right mind would sell their kids' services for profit? My mother.

~****~

God, how I hated Mondays, especially when I

didn't get enough sleep. Nikki and I ended up ordering a pizza and watching a sappy chick flick after she got off work. It was nice to have someone to do things with. It was late when she finally left. I offered her the couch, but she thought it would be better if she went home. She still had this phobia about not feeling safe. I remember the first time I went to her apartment. I couldn't believe the security measures she took. There had to be at least five deadbolt locks on her door. She also had bars on her windows, which I felt was kind of silly considering she lived on the third floor with no access to her apartment from the outside, unless you rappelled down from the roof or just so happened to be carrying a forty-foot ladder.

Before I headed out the door, I made sure Oliver had plenty of food and water. He was almost like not even having a pet; the majority of his time was spent laying around. Tucking what I needed in my purse, I grabbed my sweater and left my apartment. I was running a little late and was thankful that the traffic wasn't too bad. I was able to hail a cab quickly, which allowed me to get to the gallery only ten minutes late.

Since Lilly was away on vacation the gallery was pretty uneventful. Leave it to her to make sure I wouldn't be swamped with showings or meetings. It wasn't that Lilly didn't trust me with those tasks, it was that she preferred knowing all of her clients, present and future. Going to the back room where we kept most of our supplies and where we had a small kitchen set up, I began making a fresh pot of coffee. Just as I was walking back to the front of the gallery, I heard the bell chime letting me know someone had entered the gallery. Straightening my skirt, I looked up to find Nikki standing in the entry looking at one of abstract paintings hanging on the wall.

"Nikki, what are you doing here?" I asked.

"I thought I would stop by before I went to work. I thought that we could grab lunch," she said, looking at the art on the wall.

"I don't think I can break away for lunch. How about we have lunch here? I could order something for us," I said, knowing I wouldn't be able to leave since I was the only one working.

"That would really be great. I get lunch at one o'clock. Will that work for you?" she asked.

"That would be great."

When Nikki left, I started my day by going through the invoices from the previous week. Not only was I Lilly's assistant, I was also the bookkeeper. Lilly said she trusted me to do all the accounting stuff, instead of having someone she didn't know take care of it. When she offered me a pay increase for the added duty, there was no way I could turn her down.

I was working non-stop on the invoices and I didn't notice what time it was getting to be, at least not until the chime rang at the door. The delivery order that I placed with a sandwich shop that I knew delivered, had arrived. I handed the delivery guy the owed money along with a healthy tip and grabbed the contents from him. As soon as he walked out the door, Nikki walked in. I thought for sure they were going to plow into each other. Thankfully, Nikki moved to the side of the door so he could exit.

~****~

The rest of the week was pretty uneventful. The handful of people that came in were there only to look and not buy. It was Friday, Lilly and Peter were somewhere over the Atlantic ocean on their way back to the States. When I spoke with her, she suggested we do something fun when she got home. I didn't have much of a social life so I had her pick what to do. She wanted to do something special for me since I put in so much work while she was away. She suggested going to a night club called *Thrive.* I had heard about it, but never went. It was for the more elite crowd. I didn't think jeans and a t-shirt were exactly the acceptable attire for a place like that.

After talking with Lilly it was time to close shop. Making sure all the lights were turned off, I headed to the front of the gallery to set the alarm and lock the doors. It was still light outside, and I could feel the warmth of the air blowing on my face. As I waited for a cab to pull up, I began thinking about how I needed to get out more. Spending my time in the company of an overweight Siamese cat was not my idea of how I wanted to spend my nights. I read somewhere that book clubs and dating sites were good places to meet people. The problem with that was that neither one was my cup of tea. I wasn't much of a reader, unless smut books counted, and who knows what kind of men you would meet on dating sites. Sure, they could be good guys by their profiles, but when the date came, they were total jerks or much worse.

When I got home, my trustworthy friend was waiting for me by the door. I could always count on Oliver to give me love when I got home. I was glad to see that he was beginning to warm up to me. I wasn't sure what went on in his little head, but I was pretty sure he knew that I was his new mommy. Placing my things on the counter, I walked over to where his food bowl and water dish were to make sure that he was eating. Even though he could stand to lose a couple of pounds, I was becoming concerned with the small amount of food he ate. Satisfied that he ate at least half of his food, I headed to my bedroom to change out of my clothes and into my comfy pajamas.

Making myself a quick sandwich, I grabbed the romance novel I had been reading and headed to bed. Even though I didn't get much in the sex department, it didn't mean that I couldn't pretend it was me in the book.

'As he slipped his hands down her curvy body, she began to feel the shivers of excitement run through her. His lips pressed gently against her pert nipple, giving her the pleasure she longed for. Slipping his hand further down her body, she could feel the onset of her orgasm build. Her hips lifted as he took hold of her tight ass and placed her long silky legs over his shoulders. With a deep breath, she felt the push of his impressive cock enter her, stretching her so that she could accommodate his rod.'

"Wow," was all I could say. My body felt so hot,

I thought I was going to spontaneously combust. Placing my book on the other side of the bed, I reached under the covers and continued to fantasize where I left off. Lowering my pajama bottoms and my underwear, I slipped my finger between my slick folds. Finding my swollen nub, I began moving my finger in slow circular movements. Dipping my middle finger inside me, I curved it just enough to find the soft spongy spot in my vagina. God, how I wished it was the alpha-male in the book getting me off. I pictured him in my mind as my fingers dipped further inside. With my other hand, I took hold of my nipple and began rubbing it between my fingers, Within seconds, I was on my way to a satisfying release.

CHAPTER THREE

Sabrina

Even though I had slept like a baby, my body was protesting that it wanted more sleep. I knew I needed to get going if I was going to try and find something to wear. Maybe Lilly could help me pick something out. Pushing up to my feet, I headed to the kitchen to find my cell.

"Hello," Lilly said, sounding like she might have been sleeping.

"Hey, , Lilly. How was your trip?" I asked.

"It was the best trip ever. You were right," she confirmed.

"About?" I said, confused.

"Peter popped the question. It was so romantic. He rented this boat. It was perfect. He even had the crew set an area on the top deck with tropical flower arrangements placed everywhere. We even had our own waiter that brought us our meal. I will never forget it," Lilly explained.

"I knew he would. You two were meant to be together. Anyway, about tonight, I was wondering if you would mind helping me pick out something to wear. My current wardrobe isn't exactly suitable for a nightclub," I confessed.

"Well, I can fix that. I'll just take you shopping. Think of it as a bonus for all the hard work you did while I was gone."

After, I hung up with Lilly, I was beginning to get excited about going out. I couldn't remember the last time I went out. Matter of fact, I don't think I have ever been to a nightclub or even dancing. That was when it hit me: I didn't know how to dance. *What if someone hot asked me to dance? What if I made a fool of myself, or worse, stepped on his toes?* I was totally screwed. I guess my only option was to sit and watch. Maybe I could learn a few basic moves.

Lilly showed up at my apartment about an hour later. We decided to make a day of it by grabbing lunch and then heading to the spa for a facial, haircut, and a makeover. After we left the spa, I felt like a different woman. My hair had been highlighted with soft red highlights and cut into layers so that it framed my oval face. My normal style was to wear my hair straight or in a pony. The hair style the cosmetologist picked out for me was perfect and it was also something I could easily manage.

By the time Lilly dropped me back at my apartment, I had five new outfits as well as a perfect dress for tonight. I also purchased a pair of four-inch black heels to go with my perfect little black dress. Thinking that I needed a little relaxation, I decided to delight myself in a bath full of lavender bubbles. Filling the tub, I could hear Oliver meowing in the background. Just as I was ready to go check on him, he was at my feet rubbing his soft body up against my leg. My only conclusion was that he missed me. Picking him up, I gave him a little attention, then set him on the other side of the door and closed him out.

Lilly and Peter picked me up around seven o'clock. Lilly was wearing a deep blue halter that hung perfectly on her slender frame. When she had tried it on at the dress boutique, I told her it looked perfect on her, like it was made for her. Even though my dress was more conservative, it fit my personality perfectly. It was still very sexy by my standards, given it had thin rhinestone straps that crossed in the back. The neckline was low, but not so low that my girls popped out. I also liked the frilly hemline, which stopped just above the knee. The dress coupled with my black hose and black heels, made the whole ensemble come together like I was ready to walk the runway.

I was in awe as Peter pulled up to *Thrive*. There was a line outside that wrapped all the way around the block. As soon as we got out of the car, I could hear the beat of the music as the bass echoed from the building. Lilly must have had some pull because when we walked up to the bouncer standing at the entrance, he allowed us to enter without waiting. When we stepped inside, I was amazed at how the energy flowed. The lights were flashing on the dance floor in perfect sync to the music. Everything about the club screamed, "Let me in!" It was no wonder that the line was so long. Evidently this was the place to be.

Lilly shuffled through the crowd like she knew exactly where she was going. Peter was holding onto her hand, while I followed behind. Lilly led us up to the second floor and stopped at the VIP area, where we were shown to our table. Taking our seats, a waiter quickly took our drink order and suggested that we double up since it might be a while before he would be able to get back to us. It was that crazy busy.

"This place is crazy," I yelled across the table where Lilly was sitting.

"I know. Isn't it great?" she replied.

"So how were you able to get us in without having to wait?" I asked.

"I know the owner really well. I helped him decorate his penthouse with my artwork. That and the fact that his wife doesn't know about his little fuck pad. If you know what I mean," she said with a little giggle.

I looked at her surprised, not knowing why she would even tell me. That was something you just don't spit out in a casual conversation. When the waiter came back with a tray full of our drinks, I took a long sip before setting my Manhattan on the table. Lilly stood and grabbed Peter by the hand, leading him to the dance floor. God, they looked so happy together. Sipping my drink, I sat alone at our table and watched the patrons bump and grind on the dance floor. Just as I was about to head to the ladies room to freshen up, I felt a light touch on my shoulder. When I looked up, I couldn't believe who was standing before me.

"Cop, what are you doing here? I thought you were away on a mission," I said, surprised by his presence.

"I was. I just got back this morning. Peter called to let me know that you would be here," he said.

As he took a seat next to me, I couldn't help but stare at him. He was gorgeous, even more so than I remembered. And the black jeans paired with a white button-down shirt and leather jacket were no help in toning down the attraction for him. "So...... are you sticking around for a while or are you off on a new assignment?" I wasn't sure what got into me to ask, but the way he looked, I wouldn't have minded seeing more of him, if he was going to stick around for a while.

"If you are wondering if I have any immediate plans, the answer is no. It will be nice to relax for a while. This last gig really did a number on me. How about we don't talk about it?" he said, looking at me intently.

"What?" I asked, wondering why he was looking at me the way he was.

"You look different. Good different. Matter of fact, beautiful," he said, smiling while taking in the rest of me.

"You look good too," I replied. "How about you dance with me?" This conversation was going to get heated if I didn't do something.

"Sure," he said, standing and taking me by the hand.

As we headed to the dance floor, I could feel his

grip tighten. Not in a bad way, more like in a possessive way, like he was letting the male population know that I was taken. When we reached the dance floor the song changed to "See You Again" by Wiz Khalid. As Cop pulled me close to him, I could smell the musky scent of his cologne. It was the sexiest scent I had ever taken in. Even though I wasn't much of a dancer, moving with him was easy. My body fell into sync with his as he moved first to the right for one beat and then to the left. Leaning my cheek against his broad shoulder, I took him in. There was no mistake, I was thoroughly absorbed by his existence.

He must have been feeling the same because he pulled my body even closer to his. I could feel the warm breath of his mouth on my forehead as he gently placed a chaste kiss near my temple. This man knew exactly what to do. I knew that in a matter of seconds the wetness between my legs would soon have my lacy panties drenched with desire.

It didn't matter that the song ended, neither one of us could let go. It was only when the next song was more upbeat that we broke out embrace. Looking up at Cop, I confessed, "I'm not much of a dancer, is it okay if we sit this one out?"

Cop didn't say a word, he only took hold of my hand and led me back to our table. Or so I thought. Instead, he took me to the back exit. Once we were out of the building, I stopped, jolting Cop from moving forward. "Where are we going?" I asked.

"Any place but here," he said.

"Cop, wait. We have to let Lilly and Peter know that we left,"

Pulling his cell from the pocket on the inside of his leather jacket, he looked up Peter's number and began typing a message. Raising his head from the screen on his cell phone and looking at me, he said, "Now they know."

It wasn't long before we were in Cop's truck and pulling out of the parking lot. I didn't know what it was with the alpha-male types needing big trucks, but getting inside one wasn't exactly the easiest thing to do with four-inch heels and a frilly dress. It only took a moment before Cop saw my apprehension as I tried to get in, and he swooped me in his arms and lifted me onto the seat. Reaching across my body, he took hold of the seat belt and secured it.

As he climbed in, I began to wonder where it was that he was going to take me. We were going in the wrong direction to my condo. Unable to keep quiet any longer, I asked, "Can I ask where we are going?"

"No place in particular. I just wanted to spend some alone time with you where there wasn't any noise," Cop replied.

We were quite a ways out of the city when Cop turned on a dirt road that led us through some rough terrain. I just sat back and enjoyed the ride as he maneuvered the truck around the sharp turns. We finally came to a stop at a cliff area that overlooked the city of Manhattan. All I could think about was how many people knew of this place and how many kids made out at this very spot.

When Cop turned off the engine and there was dead silence, the moment started to become very awkward. It felt almost like being on a first date and not knowing what to say in fear that it might come out stupid and embarrassing.

Unbuckling my seatbelt, I reached for the door handle and slid off the seat into the cool night air. As I stepped to the edge of the cliff, a gust of wind caught me off guard as it lifted my skirt for Cop to see my ass cheeks. Smoothing down the silky material, I felt the warmth of Cop's leather jacket being placed on my shoulders. I couldn't help but take in his scent as the breeze filled the air with the scent of musk and spice. Pulling the jacket tighter around me to keep the chill out, Cop wrapped his arms around my waist and pulled me closer into his chest.

"This is my favorite spot to come to when I have a lot on my mind," Cop confessed.

"I can see how you would come here. It is very quiet. A person could get lost in their thoughts," I replied.

"When I was a kid, I used to ride my bike up here and just sit and wonder about all the people and what they were doing at that very moment. Sometimes I would even pretend that I lived in that building," he said as he pointed in the direction of the Empire State Building.

"You dreamt that you lived in The Empire State Building?" I asked, amused.

"Yeah. Only I didn't know its name at the time. I remembered thinking how beautiful it looked at night when all the lights were on display."

Looking out over to the Empire State Building, I could understand how Cop would love that particular building. It was pretty spectacular when it was all lit up.

Taking me by the hand, Cop led me back to his truck and helped me inside. Starting the engine, he said, "It's getting late and I need to get you home."

Being with him, I didn't want this night to end, even though I knew he was right. It was getting late. It was just that I felt really comfortable with him and I wanted to know everything there was to know about him. So when Cop reached my building, I couldn't help but ask, "Do you want to come up for a minute?"

At first I thought that he was going to refuse, but then he said, "Yeah," just like that, plain and simple.

I suggested that he park in the covered garage instead of on the street. So when he pulled inside, I directed him to my designated parking spot, which I knew would never be occupied by me. Cop cut the engine, got out and walked around the front of his truck to assist me out.

When we got to my place, just like clockwork, Oliver was waiting at the front door. It didn't take him

A.L. Long

long to begin meowing and rubbing up against my leg. Cop tried to pet him, but Oliver would not have anything to do with him as he began to hiss at him. "Oliver," I scolded as he looked up at me, knowing that I wasn't the least bit happy about his behavior. "Be nice to Cop. He just wants to pet you."

Not even my words of warning could convince Oliver to be nice. He sauntered off in the direction of my bedroom meowing all the way.

"Sorry about that," I said.

"That's okay. Me and cats never seemed to hit if off. When did you get a cat anyway? I don't ever remember you having one."

"I didn't. I kind of adopted Oliver when Mrs. Jensen passed away. I just couldn't stand him being taken to a shelter. I know what happens to unwanted pets. Can I get you something to drink? I think I have wine, if that's okay?"

45

"That will be fine," Cop replied

As I grab two glasses and the bottle of wine I had in my fridge, I walk over to the couch where Cop had made himself comfortable. I handed Cop the corkscrew and watched as he masterfully uncorked the bottle of wine. When the cork popped from the bottle, my attention was brought back to the sound rather than on Cop's muscles, which were bulging through his white button-down shirt.

I knew he could feel my eyes burning into his body. There was a slight curve to his mouth as he acknowledged my attraction to him. Holding up the half full glass of wine to me. I took it slowly from him. More than anything I wanted to down the entire contents, but knew it would only confirm what he already knew. Taking a very ladylike sip, I placed the glass on the small coffee table and turned my gaze to the window in my living area.

"I just love how the city looks at night," I confessed, trying to tame down my desire for this man.

"It is a beautiful sight," Cop replied, setting his glass on the table and walking towards the floor-to-ceiling window.

Trying to figure out what he must be thinking, I watched as he leaned his hand against the glass and looked out into the city lights. Nothing could have prepared me for what he said as he turned towards me. "Sabrina, you are a very attractive woman, and right now at this very minute all I want is to strip every piece of clothing from that beautiful body of your's and put my cock so deep inside you until the only sound coming from those perfect lips is you screaming my name."

I was so focused on him, that I only heard half of what he just said. I did manage to hear "cock," "deep," and "scream." It was only after he had me up from the couch and pressed against the window that my reality finally kicked in and I knew what he wanted.

CHAPTER FOUR

Cop

Never had a woman made me come so undone as Sabrina did. I wasn't sure what had gotten into me. All I knew was that I wanted her and I couldn't stop what I was doing. Even when I picked her up and pushed her body against the window, it didn't matter that I may have been a little rough with her. Her soft moan just made me want her that much more instead of pulling back from her. It was only after her arms wrapped around my neck that I knew she wanted what I was offering.

Pressing my lips to hers, I took in her softness as I urged my tongue between her parted lips. As I caressed her tongue with mine, I could feel the vibration of her moans spread from her lips to mine. Pulling her even closer, I lifted her body, placing my hands on her ass beneath the smooth material of her dress. She should have never been allowed to wear that sexy dress. Every man in that club had their eyes peeled on her mouthwatering breasts and tight ass. I was wound so tight, the only thing that saved me was that they were only looking and not touching.

Breaking me from my thoughts, Sabrina's hands began moving down my back, where she lifted the hem of my shirt to gain access to my heated skin. God, just the feel of her touching me made my cock rock solid. Unable to take any more, her dress was up over her head in one swoop, and her firm breasts were now bare and waiting for me to devour them. Lowering my head, I placed my mouth over her taut nipple and began taking in her softness. The heat inside my pants was going to ignite if I didn't plant myself deep inside her. Twisting our bodies, I pulled her from the window and whispered, "Bedroom?"

Her soft voice rang, "Down the hall to the right," as I pulled her closer and began carrying her in that direction. Kicking the door open with my foot, I walked through the open door and placed her gently on the frilly pink comforter on her queen-sized bed. There was just enough light shining through her bedroom window that I could see the silhouette of her body as she was spread across the bed. She was even more beautiful, if that was even possible. Her body had curves in all the right places and her breasts were the most gorgeous mounds of perfection that I had ever seen. It was only when I was standing before her, taking in her beauty, that I noticed the faint line which looked to be a scar, running from the center of her stomach and disappearing around her side. It could have been something that happened long ago, based on the slight imperfection that was barely noticeable.

I began unbuttoning my shirt. Frustrated after the first few buttons. I gave up and pulled it over my head.

It wasn't long after that my boots and jeans were off. Sliding up over her, I propped my elbows on either side of her head and once again placed my lips on hers. Her mouth opened wider for me letting me, taste more of her sweetness.

Holding my body above her with one arm, I began caressing the soft flesh of her breast with the other. Tweaking the velvety firmness of her nipple, her back began arching up from the bed. There it was again, the soft moan letting me know she was about to unravel with sheer pleasure. I removed my lips from hers and began moving my way down her body. Lowing my hand, I slid it between our bodies in search of her inner warmth. Reaching the apex of her womanhood, I could feel the heat radiating between her legs. Lowering my hand further, I slid my hand under her lacy panties and placed the palm of my hand on her pelvic area while I slowly worked my finger between her slick folds. She was so wet that it was easy for me to slip my middle finger inside.

Lifting my head, I gently placed tender kisses on

her lips while whispering, "I need to be inside you, Brie. I don't have a condom, but I'm clean. Are you on the pill?"

Something wasn't right, I was so consumed by her that I didn't realize that she had become completely stiff on me. Taking in her beauty, I could see something in her eyes. It was fear. Never had I seen such a terrified look before. "Sabrina, what's wrong?" I asked, concerned as I waited for her to respond.

"I thought I could do this, but I can't," she said, pushing me away.

"What's going on, Sabrina?" I asked, demanding an answer.

"I can't. I think it's better if you left."

"Not without an answer as to what just happened."

Before I could get anything else from her, the

door to the bathroom closed and I could hear the lock engage. Walking to the door, I tapped lightly. "Sabrina, whatever is going on, I need to know," I demanded.

"Please, Cop, just go away," she replied.

There was nothing else I could do. I could hear the crack in her voice as she said those last words. I knew that she was crying behind the door. "This isn't over, Brie. I'll leave… for now."

The ride to my home in the country left me confused and pissed off. I tried to figure out what could have caused Sabrina to react the way that she did. I was so turned on by her, I thought I was going to lose it before I had a chance to really feel her. When I left her condo, I had never wanted to beat someone as much as I did then. I needed to punch something fast and hard.

Turning up the long dirt road to my little piece of heaven, I could feel the pain between my legs begin to take its toll. I had never experienced a case of blue balls in my life. I needed relief before I wasn't going to be able to walk. Unable to hold on any longer, I pulled my truck to the side of the long road and did the one thing I hadn't done since I was a teenager. Never had a woman left me in this condition before.

When I was finally able to get some relief, I put the truck back into drive and headed up the road. My log-style cabin came into view, the cabin that I spent a decade building. At home, I put everything I had into building. To most people it would have been a dream home with its big arched window overlooking the small lake that me and my dad spent many days fishing at. I never thought I would be able to rebuild a home on this land once the old house burned to the ground. Too many bad memories of the night it caught on fire. I guess that is why it took me ten years to rebuild what was destroyed all those years ago.

Pulling the truck in the three-car garage, I put it in park and headed inside the empty house. Throwing my keys on the granite counter, I decided I needed to punch something more than I needed a shower. Taking the steps to the second floor two at a time, I headed to the master to change into something more comfortable for what I had in mind. Changing and grabbing what I needed, I headed down the stairs to the basement where I built the ultimate workout room. As I entered the room, I could see my 100 pound punching bag waiting to take a beating. Slipping on my gloves, I began hitting the bag with slow steady jabs. The more I thought about what happened with Brie, the harder my punches got. Without even realizing it, the anger began to swell and my legs began doing a number as well on the bag.

My arms and legs began to burn like none other as I continued my assault on the bag. When my body was completely exhausted and no longer able to move, I removed my gloves, only to find that the protection did nothing for my knuckles. They were fire red and burned like a son of a bitch. All that abuse I did to my body had no effect on my anger.

After taking the coldest shower, I could stand, I was finally able to see clearly. Even though I put my body through hell, I knew that I needed to find out what was going on with Brie. I cared for her too much to just let this go. The only problem was that I had no way of getting in touch with her, and heading back to her place wasn't the best option at this point. I knew if I did go to her, she would just push me away. It was then that I decided to give it a rest until tomorrow. Wrapping a towel around my waist, I headed to the kitchen for a much-needed beer. There was one thing good about living out in the country with the nearest neighbor over a mile away: I could run around bare-ass naked if I wanted to.

Grabbing a cold one from the fridge, I opened the sliding glass door leading out to the deck and took a seat on the lounger. Looking across the lake, watching the stars bounce off the small ripples, I thought about how much fun I used to have on that lake fishing and swimming. God, how I missed my dad. I didn't have too many memories of my mom, except the ones my dad told me about and the ones I use to dream about. Even those were slowly fading. My dad had been the only person in my life for so long that I couldn't even remember the day my mom died or what she looked like. Since everything was lost in the fire, there were no pictures to keep her memory alive.

CHAPTER FIVE

Sabrina

What was the matter with me? Why did I keep doing this? I thought I was done with these stupid panic attacks. Now, after all this time, they decided to come back. It's been ten years since my last attack. I never had this bad of an attack with Sean. Of course, we never got past second base. Our relationship ended the day he showed his true colors and whaled on me the day he saw me talking to some guy at the community college where we met. He didn't even let me explain that I was just giving the guy directions to the admissions office before he laid into me at his apartment. He kept telling me he didn't mean to hurt me, but that was only after I wouldn't drop the charges against him. Even after what he had done, he still managed to get off easy by enlisting in the military. The judge thought it would be a good way for him to learn some anger management skills. In the mean time, I was healing from two broken ribs, a shattered wrist, and numerous cuts and bruises.

After using the breathing exercise from my old psychologist that the state had assigned me, I pushed myself from the floor and tried to pull myself together. Unlocking the door, I slowly pulled it open. I hoped that Cop listened to me and left. The last thing I wanted to do was to explain to him what was going on with me. It would only mean that I would have to go into the whole sordid deal of my life, which meant my past, and I wasn't ready to go there.

I wasn't sure what time it was, but I knew that it was late. As I stepped out of my room and into the kitchen, I could see that the time on the microwave read

1:05. Thankful that it was Sunday, tomorrow, I got a quick drink of water and headed back to my room. I was still pretty much naked except for the robe I grabbed from behind the bathroom door and the lacy panties I still had on. Pulling open the drawer of my nightstand, I pulled out the shirt and shorts that I had placed inside. Feeling emotionally drained, I climbed under my covers and pulled them over me. Trying to find a comfortable spot was nearly impossible since the minute I closed my eyes, all I could see was the look on Cop's face when I told him to leave.

Knowing there was no way I was going to be able to sleep. I pulled my book from the same drawer and flipped through the pages to where I had left off. Staring at the black and white page, reading the same line over and over, I knew it was time to give up on the book idea as well. Nothing had ever made me feel this way. I could always shake what was bothering me off and at least get some sleep. Desperate times require desperate measures. Sliding out of bed, I went to the bathroom to get the only thing I knew would help me sleep. It had been a while since I had taken a Xanax. I didn't like taking them, but when I couldn't sleep, it was the only thing that helped.

~****~

Waking up, I remembered why I stopped taking that little blue pill. My head felt foggy and I still felt like I needed more sleep even though it was already eleven o'clock in the morning. "Shit," I said as I jumped from the bed. I had about fifteen minutes to get dressed and out the door in order to meet with Tyler, my self-defense instructor. I wished I hadn't agreed to meet with him today. He had a change in his schedule and it was the only day he could manage without missing a session. Grabbing my phone and my small gym bag, I locked my door and headed down the street to the subway station.

When I finally got to the gym, Tyler was already there talking to some bimbo in tight yoga pants and a sports bra that barely covered her large fake breasts. Walking up to him, I gently tapped in on the shoulder. Once I got his attention away from the fake tan Barbie, I asked, "Ready to show me some moves?"

The expression on Barbie's face was priceless. If she only knew that Tyler was only my self-defense instructor. Turning my body and putting a little swing to my hips, I followed Tyler to the private instruction area of the gym. As I began to stretch, Tyler began preparing for our lesson. I wasn't sure what the purpose of a ball cap, a pen, and a small flashlight were with regards to our class, but I left it to him. After all, I was pretty sure he knew what he was doing.

"Okay, let's get started," Tyler said, taking his place on the mat. "First, let's go over what we've learned, then I will show you some defense tools that can also be used for protection against your assailant."

As we ran though the self-defense moves I had learned, I kept thinking about what happened with Cop. I knew sooner or later he would press me for what happened. Unable to concentrate on anything else, Tyler lifted my 128 pound body completely off the floor and planted it against the hard mat. I really needed to concentrate on what I was doing, otherwise Tyler would be getting the best of me. Straddling my hips and holding my hands above my head, Tyler had me pinned down with no way to escape. It wasn't until he let go of my arm and clenched his hands around my neck in a chocking position that I remember my next move. Taking the heel of my right leg, I secured his left ankle inward. I placed my left hand on his left wrist and turned my body. Tyler lost his balance, allowing me to push upward from underneath him. Even though he was stronger and heavier than me, I was able to get him to his back where I pretended to hit him in the groin with my fist.

"Good escape, but you should have been able to defend yourself before it got to that point," Tyler confessed.

When I held out my hand to assist him up, he quickly pulled me back to the mat and once again straddled my body. I had never seen that look on him. He wasn't in the defense mode any longer. It was something different. When he began lowering his head towards mine, I could feel something inside me that I didn't want to feel. Turning my head to avoid what I knew was happening, I looked at the mirrored wall and said, "What's the gadgets for?"

Tyler looked over to where I was looking and said, "Protection tools." Lifting off of me, he walked over to the three items and began explaining what each item was and how to use them for protection.

By the time my class was over with Tyler, I felt weird. He had never come on to me before. The first time, when he had me pinned, I thought it was just an awkward moment. But when he placed the cap on my head and brushed his hand across my cheek, it was a definite come on. I wasn't sure if I could continue seeing him as a trainer. The last thing I needed was to feel uncomfortable around him. It wasn't like he wasn't good looking and had a great body, it was just that I had enough to deal with in the male gender department. Somehow I needed to let him know that it may be a good idea if I found a different trainer.

Just as I stepped out of the gym, my phone began

to ring. Looking down on the screen, I could see that Lilly was calling. "Hey, Lilly, what's up?" I asked as I kept walking.

"What are you doing right now?" She asked.

"I was on my way home. Why?"

"I thought we could do lunch."

"Sure, can you give me about an hour? I just finished at the gym and need to shower."

"No sweat," she began to giggle, "How about I meet you at your place in about an hour?"

I hurried my pace so that I could catch the next train to my street. If I knew Lilly, she would be right on time. Entering the subway, I took a seat next to an older gentleman reading the *New York Times*. Passing the time, I looked down at the screen on my phone and noticed I had a new text. It was from a number I didn't recognize. Hesitantly, I opened the text message. It was from Cop. Staring at the message, I kept wondering how he got my number.

Cop: Things didn't end well last night. We really need to talk.

Me: How did you get my number?

Cop: Lilly. Can we please talk?

My finger hovered over the N and the Y keys. I didn't know what I wanted to do. I knew that if I answered 'yes' he would want a full explanation of my panic attack. If I answered 'no' he would want to know why, and I didn't want him to think this had anything to do with him. I knew I needed to let him know something, so instead of a 'yes' or 'no,' I typed in a hesitate 'maybe' and turned my phone off.

Getting to my condo, I hurried and got out of my workout clothes and headed to the shower. I only had thirty minutes before Lilly would be knocking on my door. Quickly washing my hair, shaving my legs and armpits, I looked down to see that my pubic area was going to need attention soon. As I turned off the water, I heard a knock at my door. *"No way could Lilly be here already,"* I said to myself, grabbing the towel I laid on the counter next to my phone. Sure enough, my thirty minutes and then some had passed. I didn't realize I had been in the shower that long. Pulling my robe down from the back of the door, I slipped it on and hurried to the door.

As always, when I opened the door, Lilly stood before me looking like she just stepped out of a magazine. Today she was wearing a pair of coral cropped pants, a coral and black silk blouse which tied at the neck, and black pumps with a coral bow in the back. I wondered if she would be willing to help me pick out an outfit for our lunch date.

"I don't think I'm early, so why aren't you dressed yet?" she asked.

"I was waiting for you to help me pick something eye catching to wear," I lied.

"Well, show me what you have."

My closet was mostly filled with jeans and t-shirt style shirts. I never had any reason to really dress up other than to go to the gallery. Even then, I mostly wore black jeans and the only four choices I had for dressy tops. Thumbing through my wardrobe, I could tell that Lilly hadn't seen anything so pathetic. When she found something she thought was suitable, she held it up to my body and rolled her eyes. Placing the clothing back, she started the process all over again. After about ten tries, she finally found something that she was happy with. She chose a pair of cream-colored tapered pants that laced up on the bottom along with a yellow and cream striped knit top. The only flats I had were black, so she offset the black with a black beaded necklace.

When I looked at myself, I had to admit that I looked pretty good. Pushing me to the bathroom, Lilly began working on my makeup and hair. The things she did to my hair and face confirmed why she chose art as a career. By the time she finished with me, my eyes popped and my lips appeared more plump than normal. My hair was pulled away from my face in a half bun, letting more of my face show. This was a whole different look for me. I wish that I had her at my beck and call to make me look this way every day.

~****~

When we got to the restaurant, our table was already waiting for us. Lilly must have called ahead of time to make the reservation. I couldn't believe that we got lucky with how packed the restaurant was. As we sat down the waiter placed our cloth napkins in our laps and opened our menus for us as he handed them over. It was very classy. Expensive too, I guessed. When the waiter returned with two glasses of Sangria, we placed our order. We both ordered light, choosing the orange and almond salad with Asian dressing and a side of grilled shrimp.

We were both enjoying our lunch when the last person on earth that I wanted to see stepped up to our table. I could tell there was something wrong about him.

Sean was usually very particular about his appearance, but today he looked like he tied one on. As he began to speak, my hunch was right.

"Hey precious, mind if I join you," he said, slurring his words.

"Sean, you need to leave. You aren't supposed to be near me," I said with gritted teeth trying to keep my voice down so I didn't cause a scene.

"That's all you ever say to me, Brie, honey. Don't you know how much it hurts me that you don't want to be near me?"

"That's because I have a restraining order on you. If you don't leave, I am going to have to have you removed, and that wouldn't be a good thing," I said, looking down at my plate so he couldn't see how nervous I really was at him being here.

Just when I thought things couldn't get any worse, Lilly chimed in, "Look buddy, Brie asked you to leave. I think you better do as she asked or…"

"I didn't ask for your opinion, bitch, so keep your big mouth shut," Sean seethed.

The waiter must have seen what was going on because no sooner than Sean said those words, the manager and two big guys were standing right behind him. Without saying a word, the two men grabbed Sean by the arm and escorted him out of the restaurant. Every person within eye shot was looking at us. I had never been so embarrassed in my life. Reaching across the table, Lilly placed her hand over mine and said soothingly. "If you want, I can get Peter to make sure he never bothers you again."

"Thanks, Lilly," I began, placing my other hand over hers, "I need to take care of this myself. Tomorrow I will go down to the station and file a formal complaint. Maybe a few days in jail will do him some good."

After we left the restaurant and Lilly dropped me off, I knew there was no way that I could go to the police and tell them that Sean had violated the restraining order. I knew the minute he got out, he would be after me for making my complaint against him known. I wished there was a way I could get him to leave me alone without ending up hurt in the process.

CHAPTER SIX
Sabrina

I wished I had one more day to relax and figure out what I was going to do about my predicament. There was no way, taking the day off would be possible considering there was so much stuff to be done at the gallery, and being it was Lilly's first day back from her trip, I knew she would have a full day of work for me to do. Drudging out of my bed, I headed to the bathroom to begin my daily routine. Looking over to Oliver, I wondered what it would be like to live the life of a cat.

When I got to the gallery, Lilly was already busy at work. I thought for sure I would be here before she did. Peeking my head in her office, I said, "I was just going to go across the street and grab some coffee and bagels. Do you have any preference?"

"I don't, but before you go, do you have a few minutes to chat?" Lilly asked, taking her hands off of the computer keyboard.

"Sure," I said as I took a seat in one of the leather chairs in front of her desk.

"I wanted to talk to you about yesterday at the restaurant. I wanted to make sure you were okay," Lilly began pushing slightly from her desk. "Your ex has some major anger issues. I really think you should report him."

"I can't do it, Lilly. If I do, he will just come after me, and it won't be just words he will use to hurt me."

"You need to do something, Brie. You can't let that jerk control your life like that," Lilly said, concerned.

"I know, Lilly. I'm just stuck. I'm damned if I do and damned if I don't."

"Let me talk to Peter and see if there is anything he can do. Have you let Cop know what's been going on?" Lilly asked.

I didn't even know what to tell her. All she knew was that Cop and I left *Thrive* together. She didn't know about the what happened after we left. "I haven't said anything to Cop about Sean. I don't want to bring him in the middle of my problems. Please let me handle this, Lilly," I pleaded.

"Okay, only if you promise one thing. If Sean continues to harass you, promise me you will let Cop know."

Nodding my head, I pushed up from my seat and

said, "Okay, I will. Promise."

Heading out the double doors, I thought about what Lilly asked of me. The only thing that I could hope for was that Sean would leave me alone. It would be stupid of him to keep coming to me with a restraining order against him. That was when I decided to make a promise to myself. Three strikes, he's out. The next time he came close to me, I would let the police know.

~****~

The remainder of the week went by without a hitch. Lilly and I mostly worked on the upcoming showing of a new artist that Lilly met while she and Peter were on vacation in the Bahamas. She worked on the art display while I contacted the media to let them know the dates of the showing. By quitting time Friday, I was ready to just go home and soak in a nice hot bath. Lilly had invited me to go with her and Peter for drinks, but I told her that I needed to pass because I just wanted to relax and watch a sappy movie. Thank God, she didn't push me to go with them. She must have seen how exhausted I was.

God, how I hated riding the subway. There was always so many people shoving and pushing to get where they needed to go. Sometimes it made me feel claustrophobic the way everyone pushed their way inside the subway car. It was especially worse when I got off work. I really needed to get a car. After an excruciating ride, I finally made it to my condo. As soon as I unlocked the door, I knew something was off. Normally Oliver would be lying on the cushion below the window between the kitchen and the living area. Getting a little concerned, I began calling for him. "Oliver, here kitty, kitty."

When he didn't come to me, I started to search for him. It was only after I could hear him crying that I began to tune my ears to where his cry was coming from. His pleading cry led me to my bedroom, where his wailing became louder. As I stood still and listened again, I could tell that it was coming from my closet. As I opened the door, he flew out so quickly that I missed seeing where he went. The way he ran from the closet, he seemed terrified of something. Scanning the closet for anything that could have triggered his behavior, I came up with nothing.

Before I had a chance to seek him out, there was a knock at my door. Glancing over to his favorite spot under the window, I felt relieved that he had settled down. Focusing back to the door, I opened it, only to be pushed back, causing me to stumble backwards. The look in Sean's eyes was the look of someone who was ready to kill. I knew that look all too well. Scrambling to my feet, I tried to get to my cell, which was in my bag that I placed on the counter. Sean was too fast. He grabbed my legs and began pulling my body towards him. It didn't matter how much I tried to fight him. The strength he had was triple what mine was.

When he had me where he wanted, he picked me up from the floor by my hair and threw me on the couch. God, how I wished that Oliver was a large pit bull and would bite the shit out of him. Sean walked up to me and once again grabbed my hair in the back of my head. His voice was deep and evil. "You should have treated me differently at the restaurant, Brie. I think it's time you learn some manners on how to treat your man."

"Why are you doing this, Sean? Why would you think that I want any part of you?" I yelled.

"Oh, baby, don't you know. I will never let you go. The only way you're going to know that is if I remind you."

Just as he spat his sick confession, his fist landed on my cheek, causing my head to go spinning. I covered my face with my arms, but that only exposed my body, which he was now hitting instead. It didn't matter what part of my body I tried to protect, he was getting to me from all angles. It was only after he planted his last punch across my face that I thanked God for letting me go under.

I wasn't sure how long I had been out. My body hurt in so many ways that I couldn't move in order to see the display on the microwave. Oliver settled his body on the end of the couch looking at me like I was an alien from a different planet. "Thanks for the help," I choked. As much as it pained me, I knew I needed to make myself get up from the couch and get to my cell phone. Unable to stand, the only option I had was to crawl there. Halfway to where my bag was, there was another knock on the door. There was no way I could make it there. Giving it everything I had, I yelled, "Help."

I had never been more thankful to see Cop standing there as he opened the door. The breath I was holding finally left my body and my head hit the floor. I could hear his footsteps come towards me. "Oh God, Brie, what the fuck? Who the f....?"

He must have seen the look on my face. Before he could finish cursing, his arms were under my body lifting me back to the couch where he gently placed me. While going in and out, I could hear bits and pieces of the conversation he was having on the phone. If I had to guess, he was either talking to the police or one of the guys from Jagged Edge Security.

When the paramedics arrived along with the police, I knew it must have been the police he was talking with. As the paramedics took my vitals, I could hear Cop in the background explaining what he knew about what happened. I knew he couldn't tell them much, considering he arrived after Sean's assault on me had happened. If he would have been just here just a little sooner, maybe he would have been able to stop Sean from beating the crap out of me. Maybe it was time that I let him know what was going on. I couldn't tell him the whole story about my past, but maybe I could let him know about the relationship with Sean Bishop.

After an uncomfortable two hours in the ER being poked and prodded, I was finally taken to a private room. The last time I spent any time in a hospital was the day that Sean beat the shit out of me two years ago. Before that, the only other time I was in a hospital was ten years ago when I almost lost my life.

The nurse hooked me up to some monitors and

made sure my IV fluids were at the right drip level. Just as she was leaving, Cop was coming into the room. There were a few words exchanged between them that I couldn't hear. Cop pulled out a chair that was in the corner of the room and placed it close to my bed before he took a seat. Taking my hand into his and pulling it to his lips, his eyes never left mine. I had a pretty good idea what he was going to say so instead of letting him talk, I began to spill. "I know what you're going to say. I haven't said anything to you, because I didn't want to involve you in my problems."

"Sabrina, you need to tell me now what happened. Whether you like it or not, I just became involved," he asserted.

Taking a deep breath, I began explaining. "I was dating a guy I met my senior year in college. He was really nice. Anyway, I found out what he was really like. He got jealous when he saw me talking to a guy. He wouldn't let me explain that I was only giving him directions. I thought that everything was fine until we got back to his place and he began whaling on me. I ended up in the hospital. I filed charges against him, which only landed him in the military. I thought he was done with me until he began harassing me a couple of months ago. I guess the weight of a restraining order means nothing to him."

"I wish you would have let me know, Sabrina. I could have made sure this wouldn't have happened to you," Cop said, rubbing his thumb across the back of my hand.

"I know I should have. I just thought he would never come after me again."

"I know you aren't going to like what I have to say, but I think it might be a good idea if you didn't go to your condo," Cop began, stopping as he looked over to my reaction. "Sabrina, he knows where you live, and since he only sees the restraining order as a useless piece of paper, you would be safer with me at my place until he can be brought in."

I knew that Cop was right. I would be stupid not

to listen to him. I was done getting the shit knocked out of me. Nodding my head, I said, "Maybe it would be safer if I didn't go back to my place, at least until I can find a different place to live."

"Good. The nurse said that they want you to stay here overnight, just for observation. Your lucky you didn't end up with a concussion or broken ribs," Cop said as he stood to pull his phone from his pocket. "I'm going to get in touch with Peter and let him know what happened. I want to find this motherfucker before the cops do."

As Cop left to make his call to Peter, I kept thinking about what he said. He was probably right. My situation could have turned out a lot worse than it did. It made me wonder why Sean didn't just lay into me like he did the last time.

CHAPTER SEVEN

Cop

Seeing Sabrina lying on the floor helpless, bloodied the way she was, just about made me lose all control. I could feel my chest tighten as my throat began to contract. Her lying there reminded me so much of Sarah. Only with Sarah, I was too late. Looking back at that day, the reason we had fought and I stormed out of the apartment was so stupid. Who even cared if she wanted my father to be at the wedding and I didn't? After all, he was the only family I had even though we weren't on the best of terms at the time. One thing about Sarah, she always saw the best in everybody. Even though I knew she could do better, she reminded me everyday that I was a good person and that one day I would make a difference in the world. Even though I didn't love her I still miss her.

Pushing back my thoughts, I began to focus on the matter at hand, Sabrina. I would never be able to understand why she would choose to get beat up instead of telling me about her ex. No man should ever lay a hand on a woman. In my book, they deserved to be removed from God's green earth and put somewhere where the sun never shined.

After a long conversation with Peter and getting his commitment to help me find Sean Bishop, I went back to Sabrina's room to check up on her. Opening the door, I could see that she had fallen asleep. Even with her face busted up the way it was, she was still the most gorgeous woman I had ever seen. Closing the door quietly, I headed out of the hospital to meet up with Peter to talk about a plan to find Mr. Bishop. I knew the best way to find him was to get back to the office and search our data base for police records pertaining to him. I hated leaving Sabrina, but I knew she would be safe in the hospital. I also knew the sooner I got the information I needed, the sooner I could make my way back to her.

When I pulled up to the shop, all the guys were already here. Turning off my truck, I headed inside. Just like always, Hawk was shooting pool with Sly while the rest of the guys were cleaning equipment. I didn't see Peter, but knew he was here also. Making my way to the back of the shop, I peeked my head inside Peter's office, finding him on the phone while typing something on his computer.

Resting my worn body on the chair in front of his desk, I waited for him to finish his call. As I waited, thoughts kept rushing in my head. All I could think about was making Sean the scumbag motherfucker pay for what he did to Sabrina. I could feel my hands tighten around the metal armrests of my chair. I was clutching them so hard, I was surprised that they didn't snap in two. Peter must have seen my anger as he ended his call.

"Cop," he said, trying to pull me from my angry thoughts.

"Yeah, I know," I replied.

"I just got off the phone with Richard's friend at the NYPD. He shared some information about Sean Bishop with me that could help us in locating him," Peter advised.

"What kind of information?" I knew whatever he had wasn't going to be good.

"Mr. Bishop has been in and out of trouble since the age of thirteen. His record starts with assault on a teacher, where he was sent to juvie for thirteen months. From there he got into even more trouble with gang members and dealers."

"If that's the case, I don't understand how he and Brie ever crossed paths. She said they met in college. With his background, it doesn't make sense that he would be going to college," I said, confused.

"That does seem uncharacteristic of a gang member and drug dealer. Let me see what I can come up with. In the mean time, we will do whatever we need to keep Sabrina safe. It may not hurt to look into her past and see if there is any other connection to him other than their college relationship," Peter said.

"Let me handle that part. I don't want her to think I don't trust her. I know something is going on with her other than her ex. Whatever it is, it needs to be handled very delicately."

~****~

Heading back to the hospital, I couldn't help but think about what Peter said. I just couldn't image that Sabrina had any ties to Sean Bishop before college. I knew that something triggered her panic attack last week. I had a hard time believing that it had to do with her relationship with Sean and his attack on her when they were in college, especially since it sounded like she hadn't been intimate with him.

When I got to Sabrina's room, she wasn't in her bed. My heart began to tighten thinking about all the things that could have happened here. Just as I was about to find out where she went, I could see an orderly coming this way pushing her on a narrow transportation bed. I moved out of the way so that he could maneuver inside her room. I was just about to offer my assistance in getting her back in her hospital bed when another orderly showed up. Even though I knew they were only doing their jobs, I got the feeling they were enjoying their jobs a little more than they should have.

Walking over to her bed, I could see the concern on her face. It wasn't because of her own, it was because of mine. Like a book, it was written all over my face. Breaking our contact, I turned and pulled the vacant chair closer to her bed. I knew that she was watching my every move. I needed to say something to break the discomfort I was feeling. "So where did they take you?"

"For some more tests. If I am to get out of here

tomorrow, they wanted to make sure everything is okay," she said.

"Well, at least they are taking good care of my girl." I wasn't sure what caused me to call Brie "my girl," but she was, at least where I stood with her.

"Your girl, huh," she said unsure.

"Yeah, at least I like to think you are," I replied as I took hold of her hand.

I didn't think a situation could have gotten any more awkward. Brie pulled her hand from mine. It was as if she was not only disapproving my declaration, she also confirmed that she didn't want to have any part of what I just said. Being the coward that I was, I stood from my seat and bent over to kiss her on the forehead. "It's getting late and you need your rest. I'll be back in the morning."

When she didn't say anything, I turned and left the room. I wished I could take back what I said, but I couldn't. She may not have felt the same way I did. I wanted her to know that I wanted to take things a step further with her. She was like no other woman I had ever met. Even when I left on the mission to Mexico, all I could think about was her. Then when I saw her in the sexy black dress at *Thrive*, I knew exactly what I wanted.

~****~

Reaching the comfort of my home, I pulled my truck in the garage. The first thing that I needed to do was make sure that everything would be ready for Sabrina tomorrow. Walking to my office, I booted up my computer and clicked on my surveillance app. I wanted to make sure everything was working properly. It appeared that it was. All the cameras were aimed at the right position and the images were all clear. After what had happened to Sarah, I had the security system installed. I never thought my home would be targeted, since it was far enough away from the city and off of the main road. To this day, I still believe the men who broke in and took her life were here for one thing, her. My efforts in finding her killer went cold. Nothing led to why they would have been after her. Even though we weren't in love, I felt it was my duty as a gentleman to do the right thing. After all, she was carrying my unborn son. Every time I think about it, my heart dies, knowing I would never have the chance to meet the little man.

~****~

I got to the hospital a little later than I had wanted to. When I stepped into Sabrina's room, the nurse was just finishing up with the discharge papers. I could tell by the look on Sabrina's face that she was ready to get out of this sterile environment. I was glad when another nurse showed up a short time later with a wheelchair. The tension between us could have been cut with a knife. I needed to talk to her about yesterday and get some clarification. The last thing I wanted was for her to feel uncomfortable around me.

As I help her into the truck, I could tell she was struggling to keep back the pain that was being inflicted on her body as she tried to step up on the running board. Knowing that she was in pain, I stepped up behind her and gently lifted her into the truck. With a half smile she said, "Thank you. I'm still a little sore."

"I guess I'm going to have to park the truck for a while," I confessed.

When she didn't respond, I closed the door and rounded the front of the truck and got in behind the wheel. I heard her slight moan of discomfort as she tried to buckle herself in. "Are you okay?" I asked with concern.

"Yeah, just a little sore."

Giving her a reassuring wink, I put the truck in drive and said, "Let's get out of here and get you home."

By the way she looked at me, I must have said something wrong again. It was only after I began driving that it hit me what I said, "home." It wasn't meant to throw her off. I guess I should have said cabin. Needless to say, I kept my thoughts to myself the rest of the drive. I was glad that Sabrina fell asleep five minutes into our drive to my place. It gave me time to think even more about the situation. I knew Peter and the guys were doing everything possible to find Sean Bishop, but it still wasn't enough.

Just as I pulled up to the cabin, Sabrina began to stir. I reached over and rubbed her cheek gently and said, "We're here."

"The pain medication they gave me really knocked me out. I have never been so tired," she said, as she tried to move to a more comfortable position.

"Well, let's get inside and you can rest."

Nodding her head, she unbuckled her seatbelt and reached over to open the door. I hurried out of the truck so I could assist her out. The last thing I wanted was for her to endure any more than what was absolutely necessary. Before her feet hit the dirt, I had her in my arms carrying her up the stone path to the front door. Holding on to her tightly, I reached in my pocket for the key. Once we were inside, I punched in the code to disarm the security. This was another feature I was glad I had installed.

Holding on to Sabrina, I was loving the way she felt in my arms. This was something that I could definitely get used to. I kept going back and forth on whether or not it would be a good idea to lay her down on my bed or put her in the guest bedroom. The last thing that I wanted was to make her feel uncomfortable. As much as my body wanted her near me, my common sense took over and led me to the guest room, where I gently placed her on the bed. Removing her shoes, I pulled the soft blanket draped across the end of the bed and covered her with it. The minute she was covered, she tucked her hands under her cheek and closed her eyes. Everything about her was making my dick hard. I knew I had to leave before I crawled into bed beside her.

CHAPTER EIGHT
Sabrina

Waking up in the darkness, I couldn't believe how much my body ached. Even though it wasn't as bad as the last time, it was bad enough that I had a hard time moving. Looking around, my surroundings were unfamiliar, but I knew that I was at Cop's place. I must have been in the guest bedroom. What I knew for sure was that I needed to pee and there wasn't a bathroom in the room that he placed me in. Struggling, I used everything I had, took in a deep breath and lifted my body from the bed. Once I was standing, it took me a moment to get my bearings in order to walk to the bedroom door. Step by slow step, I managed to make it to the door. Turning the handle, I looked down the hallway and spotted an open door. Making my way in that direction, each step was becoming more and more painful, but I had to pee more than anything. *"God, I hope that is the door to the bathroom,"* I said to myself as I gritted my teeth with each miserable step.

Finally, my efforts paid off as I sat on the cold surface of the toilet and relieved myself. I was so desperate to get to the bathroom that I neglected to lock the door. I could hear Cop's voice calling for me. The last thing I wanted was for him to open the door and see me in not one of my finer moments. Yelling at him so he would stop searching, I called, "I'm in the bathroom, be out in a sec." When I didn't hear a reply, I assumed that he had already left to look for me elsewhere. It was only after he opened the door that I found out my assumption was wrong. Trying to cover myself the best I could, I grabbed the plush towel off of the towel bar and covered my lower body. "Hey, you could have at least knocked," I said, feeling my cheeks become flush with embarrassment.

"I didn't even know you were in here. Typically a person turns on the light before they sit on the throne," he admitted as he switched the light on.

"Yeah, well, I really had to go," I confessed. "Could you please leave so I can finish with a little dignity?"

As soon as Cop left, I finished my business. It was much easier getting to the bathroom, then leaving. Grabbing hold of the counter and the handle on the shower, which I didn't notice before because the lights were off, I lifted my body from the toilet. Now I knew why the hospital insisted on having a high rise seat placed in the bathroom. Not as far to lower yourself.

As I left the bathroom Cop was waiting for me outside the door. He must have seen how much pain I was in by the look on my face, because his arms were around me lifting my body off the floor. Wrapping my arms around him without hesitation, I said, "Thank you."

Cop eased me back onto the bed and made sure I was comfortable. The ideal situation would have been to be in my comfortable pajamas, instead of the jeans and t-shirt I arrived at the hospital in. Looking down at my attire, Cop said, "I sent one of the guys to pick up a few things at your condo and check on Oliver. If you would like, I can help you to at least get out of your jeans so you are somewhat comfortable."

"I really would be more comfortable," I said as I began undoing the buttons on my jeans.

I may have made a mistake in allowing Cop to help me. The touch of his hands on my body sent a tingling sensation down my body to the apex of my sex. Just like before, all I could think about was feeling him. Looking up at me, I knew he could feel what I was thinking. Gliding his hands up my body, he slowly caressed my skin, careful not to touch my bruised areas. His touch was so tender that it was driving me crazy with desire. I wanted this man more than anything.

Placing my hand on his arm, I followed his movements, letting him know that I didn't want him to stop. Changing his position, he placed his body next to mine while still stimulating my senses with his touch. It was only when his lips captured mine that my true desire for this man emerged. The minty taste of his mouth pressed to mine, set my body on fire. I wanted him so bad at this moment that it didn't matter that my body hurt. What mattered more was the way he was making me feel.

Cop's hands slowly began moving down my side until they reached the waistband of my jeans. With a slight tug, he began gently lowering my jeans down my legs. It took everything I had to not just kick the damn things off. I knew that If I wanted more, I couldn't let him know the amount of pain I was actually in. The pain pill I had gotten at the hospital was beginning to wear off, but every tender touch of his hand somehow soothed the pain away.

With my jeans completely off, the only obstacle in the way was my lace panties. I knew they were soaked with desire. Cop wasted no time. As much as I was attached to my only pair of sexy, lacy panties, it didn't matter that he had them ripped off me in seconds. Knowing that he still wanted me after what happened between us made my heart swell. Easing off of me, he quickly removed his own clothing. Completely naked with his gorgeous body displayed in front of me, he nestled in beside me. His hands began touching me where they had left off. The warmth of his body next to mine made my body even hotter. It was only when he said, "Are you sure you want this, Sabrina?" that I knew I wanted this more than anything.

"Yes, please," I said softly.

"Okay, baby, nice and slow," he said as he moved his hands lower down my body.

The heat between us ignited as he slipped his hands between my legs. My folds parted like the Red Sea as his finger found their way inside my entrance. With a soft moan of the unexpected, I arched my back into him, letting him know that I wanted more. As he added another finger and began caressing my g-spot, I could feel the beginnings of what I knew would be the most explosive orgasm I would ever experience. The more I pushed against him, the deeper he went. Every nerve in my body surrendered to his touch. It was only when his lips tenderly began doing their magic on my taut nipples that my release flared, causing my body to burn into a raging inferno. The air echoed with my screams of ecstasy only to be tamed by the softness of his lips as he gently seized mine. It was like my body was no longer my own, but controlled by the man who would take me to places I never thought I could go again.

Taking in a deep breath, I willed my body to calm as my moment of pure ecstasy subsided. It wasn't enough, My body craved more, but could it withstand the memories that had been haunting me for so long? With everything I had, I pushed them away so that the only thoughts in my mind were what was happening right now, this very moment. It was like Cop had taken everything away as he captured my lips with his. His firm but gentle nip on my bottom lip triggered yet another spurt of hunger stemming from the tip of my tongue down to the very soul of my body. There was no other man that I would let control my body the way he did. When he eased my legs apart, I knew it was a matter of time before I would be his. The memories of my past still lingered, but the more I thought about him, the further they became buried in my mind. I could feel the tip of his cock push against my entrance, willing its way inside. The tension I was feeling slowly receded as his gentle words filled my mind. "I will never hurt you. You are the one with all the power. Just let me worship you."

Reeling in his comforting words, my body let go to let him in. "Please, Cop, save me."

No sooner had I said those words than he was inside me, caressing me with his girth, giving me what my body was unwilling to accept for so long. Every movement was like a new beginning. The deeper he pushed inside me the freer I felt. Only feeling him, I took hold of this new feeling and began pushing against him as he continued his movement. It was like nothing I had ever experienced before. "God, Brie, you feel so good. I could get lost inside your tight cunt forever."

"Then don't ever leave," I said, wanting to stay like this until there was no more life left in me.

With a little chuckle, Cop's movements began to increase. The way our bodies fit together were like the last two pieces of a puzzle coming together to paint a perfect blueprint of what was yet to come. Unable to hold back any longer, my body surged with an electric rush, causing it to shudder with blissful pleasure. It wasn't long after that I felt Cop's own explosion take over.

~****~

I could feel a slight breeze on my face as the cool air brushed against my cheek. The room was light, letting me know that it was morning. I wasn't sure what time it was, but knew it had to be early. Reaching across the bed. I felt for Cop, but came up short. Rolling over, I could see that the space he once occupied was empty. I knew I couldn't have been dreaming about what had happened last night. It was a night that I would never forget. Sitting up, I was reminded of the pain I had forgotten about only hours ago. Looking to the nightstand for a clock or anything that would let me know what time it was, I saw a small note along with two white pills and a glass of water.

Brie,

I may have gotten a little carried away last night, but by no means am I sorry. It was the most incredible night of my life. I knew that when you woke up this morning, your body would be reminded of what I can only explain as pure ecstasy. Hope I wasn't too hard on you. When you are ready, I will be waiting for you on the deck outside with a perfect breakfast.

C

Reading Cop's note made my heart sing. I was a little more sore than I had been yesterday, but every additional ache and pain was well worth the pleasure I received in the end. Pushing from the bed, I took the two tablets Cop left and popped them into my mouth. I wanted this day to be perfect, so before I actually swallowed them down, I spit the two white pills out and only popped one back into my mouth. The last thing I wanted was to be sleeping all day. I would rather cope with a little pain than to spend the day sleeping instead of spending it with Cop.

Pushing from the bed, I went to the bathroom to freshen up and relieve myself before I headed downstairs to the deck. I couldn't bring myself to put on my clothes, so I grabbed Cop's button-down shirt that he must have slung over the chair last night. It was the only clothing I had on, for the sexy lacy panties were torn off of me during our heated passion. Cop was much bigger than me, so I was glad that the shirt he left behind more than covered all my private parts.

When I got downstairs, Cop was sitting at the table outside looking very domestic reading what I assumed was either the *New York Times* or *USA Today*. As I opened the sliding glass door, his eyes automatically darted my way. I could see that beautiful smile light up his face as I closed the door and stepped towards him. As he held out his hand, I walked toward him and reached out for his. He pulled me closer, settling me on his lap, forgetting about his paper and focusing his attention on me.

As his lips gently touched the area below my ear, I could hear the soft whisper of his voice. "How are you this morning?"

They way he spoke was the sexiest thing I had ever heard. I was completely breathless as I said, "Wonderful."

Cop dipped my body so I was no longer sitting up straight, but resting in his arms. His lips came crashing down on mine and my arms had a mind of their own as they wrapped around his neck to pull him closer. The way I was feeling I knew there was no way I would ever get enough of this man. It was the difference between night and day how much he had changed me from just a week ago. Maybe Cop was the man that could take away the bad memories and fill them with good.

The kiss ended and Cop had me back in an upright position. The look on his face became very serious, which made me concerned for what was going to come next. "Brie, I think it would be a good idea if we increased the odds for your protection. There are some things that I can show you in the event you're attacked again. Not that I would ever leave you unprotected, I just want to make sure I have all my bases covered."

"Do you want to teach me self defense?" I said, looking at him intently.

"I don't think it would hurt for you to learn some self defense moves in order to protect yourself," Cop admitted.

"I am already taking self defense classes. And I am doing pretty well, I might add," I said defensively.

"What do you mean you are already taking defense classes?" he replied, confused.

"Yeah, when Sean showed up at my condo the first time, I knew I needed to protect myself. I wasn't going to let him hit me again. At least not without a fight." After I confessed those words, I realize that Cop didn't know anything about Sean's previous visit. The look on his face said it all as he placed his hands on my hips and guided me off his lap.

"Jesus Christ, Sabrina, now you bring this up? How long has this been going on? I can't believe this," he cursed sending a chill down my body. Without even thinking, I quickly moved away from him. The look in his eyes reminded me so much of the man who entered my life ten years ago. As I backed away from him, his eyes softened. "What is it, Sabrina? What is really going on with you?"

I couldn't let him know the truth, not yet. "Nothing, I need to shower," I said as I reached behind me to find the handle to the door.

Without hesitation, I needed to get away from this situation and fast. As soon as I turned the handle, the door popped open and I was inside like a bolt of lighting. The last thing I needed was to bring things up from my past to a man I only began to know. Rushing up the stairs, I headed to my bedroom to grab the only articles of clothing that I had. It didn't matter what I wore because as soon as I was showered and dressed I would be leaving. I couldn't risk Cop finding out the truth about my past. I was surprised to find that there was a small bag lying on the bed. As I unzipped the zipper, I could see that some of my personal things were inside. My only assumption was that one of the men from Jagged Edge must have brought my things from my condo while I was on the deck with Cop. Grabbing the few items that I needed, I headed out the door to the bathroom.

Just as I emerged from the bathroom, Cop was leaning against the opposite wall with his arms crossed at his chest. I wondered how long he had been standing there. It was only after I tried to ignore his presence by avoiding eye contact and heading back to my room that he stopped me by gently pulling me by the arm. My gaze immediately met his.

"We need to talk. What just happened on the deck resembled the night you told me to leave your condo. There is something else going on with you other than what happened between you and Sean. If we are going to trust each other you need to tell me what is going on."

My mind hung on every word he said. The only problem was that I couldn't begin to tell him the truth. Placing my hand over his, I gently unclenched his hand and removed it from my arm. With the strength he had, he did not resist my movement. Looking up to his still eyes. I said the one thing I could say without telling him the truth, "It's complicated and it's something I can't talk about now. I need you to take me back to my place."

"Are you crazy, Sabrina? The last place I would ever take you is back to your place. He knows where you live and I can't risk him showing up. It would be better if you stayed here for the time being," he said with sincerity.

"Okay, on one condition. I don't want you hounding me about what may or may not be going on with me," I declared.

"Okay, for now. Can you at least show me what you have learned?"

By the time I finished showing Cop everything that Tyler had shown me the best I could with my injuries, Cop was reeling in disapproval. Everything I did was either taught wrong or a useless maneuver. Dissecting every move, Cop showed me the right way to defend myself whether the attacker came behind me or approached me from the front. He made every move look so simple that when I began doing them myself, the outcome was twice as effective. I didn't regret taking classes from Tyler, but I did regret losing so much time and really learning nothing from him.

CHAPTER NINE

Cop

When Sabrina confessed to me that she had taken self-defense classes from Tyler, I just about lost it. The thought of him so much as touching her made my insides fill with rage. I knew Tyler very well. His brother and I went way back, even before we enlisted in the service together. Unlike his brother, Mac O'Connor was a good man and a good friend. He dedicated his life to the military and to the Special Forces, which very few men got the privilege to serve in. Tyler never took any discipline seriously. It surprised me when he decided to go into self-defense training after serving only one term with the Army. I guess he thought being a trainer was a great way to meet women. The day combat took Mac's life, I made a promise to him to take care of Tyler. I think he wanted me to make sure he stayed out of trouble more than anything. What happened to Mac was a grave mistake. It is something I will never forgive myself for. Only a handful of people knew what happened in that godforsaken desert: Peter, Hawk, Sly, and Tyler.

I wasn't able to show Sabrina everything that I wanted to. She was still sore from her injuries and I didn't want to inflict any more pain on her than she was already having. I couldn't believe some of the moves she had shown me. Leave it to Tyler to show her the bare minimum. My guess was that he wanted to draw out his training with her, until the day came that he could get inside her pretty lacy panties. I didn't like the way he trained, but there really wasn't anything that I could do about it. I did know one thing for certain: there was no way that Brie was going to be going back to him for instruction. All I had to do was make sure he didn't find out that I was teaching her. Tyler didn't know me as

Cop. He only knew me as Vince Coppoletti.

While Brie was up in the bathroom showering, I thought it would be a perfect time to get in touch with Peter to see if he had any more news about Sean Bishop. Waiting for him to answer, I stared out at the lake. Three rings into my call, he finally picked up. "Hey, Cop," he said.

"Hey, just checking to see if you have any more information on Sean Bishop," I asked, looking back at the door to make sure I was still alone.

"Sly is checked on a few leads. Other than that, nothing new," Peter confessed.

"What leads?" I asked, irritated that he hadn't said anything before about any leads.

"Not sure if they are going to pan out, but we may know where he might have been staying. Sly is hoping that he left a forwarding address."

I wasn't sure where Peter's thought process was coming from, but I knew that even if Sean left a forwarding address it would be bogus. Nobody would be that stupid. "Do you really think he would be that stupid?"

"I don't know, maybe. He was stupid enough to beat the shit out of Sabrina knowing he had a restraining order against him," Peter reminded me.

After I ended the call with Peter, my tension against this guy began to build even more. With no answers to speak of, I was becoming more and more irritated. Heading back inside, I went to check on Sabrina. Climbing the stairs two at a time, I headed to her room. Hopefully by tonight, she would be in my bed instead of across the hall.

I gently knocked on her door, but it wasn't closed all the way and swung open. As I entered her room, I could see she wasn't inside. The only other place she could be was in the hall bathroom. Looking down the short hall, the bathroom door was open and the lights were off. I didn't know where she went. Going to my own room, I hoped that she decided to use my shower instead. It was much bigger with pulsating jets on two sides.

When I entered my room, I could hear the shower going, which let me know that she was inside. Slowly opening the door, she was standing with her back to me. The jets were spraying her shoulders, soothing the soreness from the way her soft moans escaped her mouth. I decided to take a chance that she would allow me to share the shower with her. Removing my shorts and t-shirt, I opened the glass door to the shower and stepped in behind her. When she felt a break in the spray, she turned towards me, giving me a perfect view of her pert breasts. It was only then that I could see fully the extent of her injuries. It wasn't so much the bruising around her ribs and legs that had my eyes peeled to her, it was the thin red line that I had barely noticed a week ago. With the heat of the water, the scar was more visible. It stretched from the middle of her stomach and around the side of her waist. Placing my finger on the mark, I began tracing the scar. Just by the feel of it, I could tell that this wasn't something she would have received accidentally. The cut was clean with no jagged edges, almost like someone had done surgery on her.

Taking her focus away from my hand, I lifted her chin so that her gaze was focused on me. In a concerned tone I asked, "Brie, baby, what happened?"

Turning away from me, she responded, "An unfortunate mistake."

"Did Sean do this to you?" I couldn't help but wonder if this was part of what he did to her.

"No. Can we please not talk about this?" she said forcefully.

I didn't want to make her angry, so I let it go for the time being. Instead of saying what I really wanted, I forced her to turn towards me, then lifted her body from the shower floor and pressed her against the tile wall. Lowering my head, I captured her sweet lips. Biting her bottom lip, I urged my tongue inside, only to be greeted by the vibration of her soft whimper as our tongues began dancing together. I could feel my cock come to life as our kiss deepened. Her breasts lightly brushed my chest, sending a wave of euphoria from the tip of my toes to the tip of my hard cock. All I wanted was to be deep inside her creamy channel. With one arm holding her to the wall, I slide the other between our wet bodies and guided my shaft inside her tight entrance. I could feel her body move upwards as she let more and more of me inside. Just when I though it couldn't get any better, her body came down on me, causing my cock to be buried deep inside her. It took everything I had not to come at that moment. Her warmth felt so good wrapped around me, that I would have exploded if I hadn't been in control.

Holding on to my shoulders for leverage, Brie began moving up and down my hard shaft taking even more of me. God, the pleasure I was experiencing was beyond anything I had ever experienced with any woman. The more I pushed inside her, the more I could feel her walls tighten around me. I knew she had to be in pain the way I was pressing her against the wall. Pulling her off of me, I set her down only to turn her body quickly so that I could resume my attentions from behind. With her legs slightly spread, I easily slipped my cock between her slick folds and began pumping in and out of her. With one hand on her hips, I moved the other around her until it found its way to the center of her core. Palming her mound, I gently circled her swollen nub with my middle finger, adding to pleasure she justly deserved. Her body began pushing against mine, prompting me to go even deeper.

"Brie, you feel so fucking good, I could come right now," I moaned.

"I don't know how much longer I can hold on, Cop," she whimpered.

"Don't hold back, baby, I'm right behind you," I confessed.

As soon as her body jolted, I knew that she was met with her release. It took only a couple of more pumps and I was right there with her. I could feel my heart stop as a surge of ecstasy took over.

~****~

"Let's get out of here," I said as Brie finished dressing. I needed a reprieve. If we stayed here much longer, we would end up christening every room in my house.

"Okay, where?" she asked.

"I have a small boat, We could take a ride around the lake, maybe do some fishing," I suggested.

"Fishing?" she said, crinkling her nose.

"Come on, it will be fun," I said.

I could tell that Brie wasn't too thrilled about going fishing. If I had to guess, she had probably never been fishing in her life, the way she looked at me.

Brie made a couple of sandwiches, while I gathered everything we would need from the garage. I didn't have a fresh supply of night crawlers, but I knew exactly where I could get some. Grabbing a container and filling it with some moist dirt from the back yard, I head down the path towards the lake. There was one area where those little critters loved to hide. Moving the rocks near a large pine, I was able to capture about a dozen worms. There was enough to fill the container. Closing the lid, I could see that they were already making themselves at home.

Placing the needed items I grabbed from the garage inside the boat, I made sure that there were two life vests and paddles in case the motor quit on us while we were out. I hadn't used the boat very much since my dad died and wasn't comfortable with the engine holding out until we got back. Better to be safe than sorry. The last thing I wanted was to get in the cold water and drag us back to shore.

I could see Brie walking towards me, with a basket full of food and an extra jacket in her hand. I wasn't sure how long we would be on the water, but knew that it could get chilly, especially if the wind happened to come up. Taking the basket from Brie, I set it inside the boat and then helped her inside. She took her place in the back of the boat while I unhooked the ropes from the dock. Climbing in, I pushed away from the dock and started the motor. It took a few tries before it finally took off.

When we got to the middle of the lake. I cut the engine. I could tell that Brie had never been on the water the way she kept looking over the side of the boat trying to guess how deep the water was. Unable to contain my laughter, I said, "The water is about fifty feet deep. The perfect spot to catch a fish." The way she looked back at me, made me think that I should have lied and said it was only ten feet deep.

"What happens if we can't get back?" she asked, her face turning pale.

"That's why we have these," I said as I held up one of the oars.

She must have felt some comfort in knowing we would be able to paddle ourselves back to shore if the motor didn't start. "Come on, I'll rig up a pole for you."

"I don't even know how to fish. How about I just watch you?" she said.

"What fun would that be? All you have to do is pull them in. I'll do the rest," I said, watching the expression on her face as she crinkled her nose in disgust.

Throwing out her line, I handed her the pole and showed her how to reel it in when she got a bite. I could tell she wasn't thrilled about the idea of having to fish in the first place, but I knew once she got a bite, it would change her impression about fishing. As I got my pole ready, I glanced up every so often to see that Brie had no interest in fishing. All she was doing was looking at her nails admiring the pretty pick polish on them. It was only after I said, "Brie, you got a bite," that she shifted her focus on her pole and began reeling it in.

" Cop, help me, I think I have a shark on the other end," she yelled frantically.

All I could do was chuckle at her admission. "Brie, I can guarantee you, there are no sharks in this lake. Maybe the Loch Ness Monster." The look on her face was priceless.

"Very funny, Everyone knows the Loch Ness Monster lives in Scotland. There's no way it would be here," she said with a serious look.

The way she was looking, I couldn't bring myself to tell her that the Lock Ness was only a myth. Sitting behind her, I wrapped my arms around her pole from behind, placing my hands over hers and began reeling it in. Even though it was most definitely not a shark, it was giving even me a run for the money. I knew that it was pretty big they way it kept fighting us. I no longer cared about pulling in the fish. The only thing that I could focus on was how Sabrina's body was pushing firmly against mine. If we weren't on the boat in the middle of the lake, I would have taken her right then and to hell with the pole. The way her ass was rubbing my groin brought my cock to life. I was becoming so hard that my pants were becoming uncomfortably tight.

When we were finally able to pull the Northern Pike in using a net I had tucked under the front seat, Brie's eyes lit up with excitement as she held onto the net while I finished reeling it in. Even though I was kidding, I told her that she would have to clean it. No sooner I said those words, she flipped the net over the water and let the fish escape.

"I was just kidding, Brie. That was a great catch you just let go," I said.

"You should have said something before I let it go. There is no way I'm going to touch that slimy thing."

The sun was just about to set as we made our way back to the house. The wind had picked up a bit and the jacket didn't do much to keep Brie warm. Placing her on my lap, I nuzzled against her to keep the cold air off of her while trying to steer. One thing I knew for certain, I was going to need some relief when we got back to the house. Her lovely ass always seemed to find just the right place to rest.

CHAPTER TEN
Sabrina

Even though I wasn't much of a fisherman, I really did enjoy myself at the lake. It was no wonder Cop loved it so much out here. It was very serene and comforting. A person could definitely get lost in their thoughts. As we walked up to the path to the house, all I could think about was taking a long hot bath in Cop's over-sized tub. Getting to the house, I removed my jacket and headed up the stairs to the large bath that was calling my name. Instead of following me up, Cop decided to put everything away first and clean the only fish we, or should I say he, managed to catch. After he told me that I would be responsible for cleaning my own catch, my decision to work on reeling them in was a no brainier. I was pretty sure Cop knew about my game plan, but didn't say anything about it.

Gathering my things from the shower, I placed them on the edge of the tub while it filled with hot water. Seeing the bath crystals that were in a glass container in the corner of the tub, I opened it up and poured a generous amount under the stream. Instantly the tub began to fill with bubbles. The scent of vanilla and lavender filled the air. It was then that it occurred to me that Cop wasn't the vanilla and lavender kind of guy. That was when my stomach began to knot, thinking that there was another woman in his life.

I tried not to think about it as I undressed and lowered my body inside the massive mountain of bubbles. The heat of the water on my body immediately soothed away the soreness. It was like being in heaven and paradise all at once. The only thing that could make this moment better was to have Cop join me. Just as the thoughts left my mind, the door slowly opened and Cop appeared. He must have read my thoughts, because soon his jeans came off, along with his faded Aerosmith t-shirt. When the defined muscles of his chest and abs came into view, I was glad that my private parts were covered in bubbles. My nipples felt tight and my pussy was getting wet, and not from just the water.

Cop placed his hand on my shoulder, "Move up a bit, baby, so I can move in behind you," he said softly.

As I scooted forward, Cop slipped in behind me and pulled me back towards him once he was settled. I could feel the tingle between my legs take hold as the hardness of his cock pushed against my ass. Adjusting my hips back so that I could feel him better, a moan sounded as he wrapped his arms around me. "I could stay like this forever with you."

Leaning my head against his broad shoulder, I said, "I would love that."

His hands moved up my body, stopping just

below my breasts, where they settled. His touch was so tender, it was beginning to drive me crazy with need. Tipping my head to his, I looked up at him with glazed eyes as the pleasure he was giving me began to take hold. Leaning my way, he placed his lips over mine and began kissing and sucking my lower lip. It took everything I had to take his slow, sensual movement rather than jump his bones like I wanted to. Breaking our kiss, Cop had my body turned and straddling his like I weighed no more than a pound of sugar. I could feel the hardness of his cock between my legs. All I wanted was for him to be deep inside me. Lifting my hips, he positioned his shaft at my entrance and slowly lowered me down. I was so wet that my opening parted and his velvety rod slid inside.

He stopped for a moment to ask, "Are you okay, baby?"

Oh yeah, I was more than okay, I thought as I said, "Yes."

He resumed his movements, quenching my desire

to feel more of him. When his movements quickened and the water began sloshing over the side, I grabbed the edge of the tub to brace myself for the imminent orgasm that was ready to explode from my body. Every pump of his cock sent my body reeling in a tail spin as I got closer and closer to my release. It was only when he shifted his position slightly causing his cock to rub forcefully against my sweet spot that I could no longer hold on. Screaming his name, the portal opened, letting my juices spill coating him like white frosting on a red velvet cake.

~****~

An hour later we were out of the tub, drying each other while making sure to touch every inch of each other's body. I wasn't sure what the sleeping arrangements were after our little bout in the tub, but I wasn't going to be the one to ask. Picking up my things from the counter, I headed towards the bedroom door to retire in the guest room where I had spent the last two nights. It was only when I heard Cop's voice that I stopped.

"Where are you going, baby? I thought that you could stay with me tonight," he asked.

I didn't want him to think that I had been thinking the same thing, so I simply told him, "I was going to take my things back to my room first, and grab some clean clothes."

"Okay, hurry back. I want some more of that sweet pussy," he demanded.

Just the thought of what he had planned, made my insides tingle, which caused my clit to throb. Opening the door, I hurried down the hall to my room to put on a pair of lacy panties and a t-shirt. They were the items of clothing that were packed for me that I could consider to be sexy enough for Cop. It really shouldn't have mattered what I put on since it would soon be removed anyway. Spraying a hint of my perfume on my neck, I checked my appearance before I left the room. When I got back to Cop's room, he was already settled on the bed with his cell in his hand. He looked to be very comfortable with his back against the headboard and his body on display from the waist up.

Shutting the door, I walked over to where he was and slipped in next to him. Taking his cell from his hand, I turned it off, reached over him, and set it on the night side. Just when I was about to straddle his body, he flipped me over onto my back. With his eyes fixed on mine, I could see that he was a man on a mission, the mission being me. He lowered his lips to mine as he whispered, "I'm going to fuck you until you beg me to stop."

My heart began to pound at his words as his hands reached beneath my shirt and lifted it up and over my head, only to rest on my wrists before Cop expertly twisted the material so that my hands were bound. Rubbing his hand across my cheek, he softly asked, "Do you trust me, Brie?"

My heart was beating even faster. I tried to focus on something else. I knew it was Cop with me, but that still didn't tame down the tight feeling I was feeling in my heart. With his hand, he lifted my chin, until I was looking right at him. "Brie, you need to answer me. Do you trust me or do I need to stop?"

The last thing I wanted was for this to stop. I knew that if I backed down now, I would not be feeling him deep inside me. Nodding my head, I looked at him confidently and said, "Yes, I trust you."

"I'm just going to hold your hands above your head. If it becomes too uncomfortable for you, all you have to do is say 'red.' Do you understand, Brie?" he questioned.

Unable to get the words out, I once again nodded by head in confirmation. Feeling my apprehension, Cop lowered his lips to mine, soothing the tension that had taken residence in my chest. His scent of musk and spice comforted me as his kiss deepened. My lips had a mind of their own as they parted to allow him entrance into my cavity. His tongue gently caressed mine as his hand began kneading my breast to the point of blissful intoxication. There was something about the way he commanded my body that made every nerve inside sizzle with an electric charge stemming from the top of my head to the tip of my toes.

As he broke our kiss and began trailing kisses down my neck along my collar bone to the small valley between my breasts, I knew soon my body would not be my own. His lips continued a downward path until they stopped at the juncture if my mound, but only to take in the scent of my womanhood. My back arched off the bed as I willed Cop to continue his ministrations on my body. Every move of his mouth had been more pleasurable yet denying me of the paradise I so wanted to be taken to. It was only after his fingers dipped inside my soaked channel that I lost all control.

Lowering his mouth between my slick folds, he began lapping up my juices like he had been without the nectar too long. The more he kissed and sucked, the more my body became sensitized to the point of letting go. His efforts halted as he repositioned his body between my legs, spreading my legs wider so that he was given ample room to plunge deep inside. Looking down on my body between my pert breasts, I could see his cock in its glorious magnificence as he carefully began working it between my folds and inside my tight channel. The feeling of fullness filled me as the pleasure I longed for filled my very being. Working against him, my hips lifted from the bed mimicking the push, pull motion as he continued to push deeper and deeper inside. When he lifted my legs over his shoulder, my body gave way as the rush of release exploded without warning, coating his cock deep inside me. His spoken word said it all, "I can't hold on any longer, baby." His body began to shudder as his seed began to spill inside me.

~****~

I wasn't sure what time it was, but when I rolled over to nuzzle against Cop's strong body, he was no longer there. Pulling the sheet from the bed, I wrapped it around my body and headed out of the room in search for him. When I got to the bottom of the stairs, I could hear his voice echoing off the walls as it became louder and more aggressive. From the way he was talking, something was going on that he was not too excited about. Entering the kitchen, Cop's body was bent over the counter with his elbows on top and his head resting between his hands. He must not have heard me enter because when I tapped his shoulder, his body tensed and his arm came flying backward before he stopped the movement when he realized it was me standing behind him. "Jesus, Brie, you can't sneak up on me like that. I could have really hurt you," he said agitated.

"I didn't want to disturb your call. It sounded pretty important," I confessed.

"There's a mission in Nicaragua that they want me to head. I leave in a couple of days," he advised.

"Wait, you can't leave. What about Sean? We still don't know where he is," I pleaded.

"There will be plenty of men from Jagged Edge Security to make sure you're safe."

"I don't want them to make sure I'm safe. I want you," I said.

My morning just went from being the best morning ever to the shittiest. Even though he was kind enough to let Oliver stay at the cabin to keep me company, I couldn't understand why it had to be Cop that had to leave. Surely one of the other guys could have taken his place. They were all capable of handling the so-called mission. When my argument ended up making me even more frustrated, I turned away from Cop and headed back upstairs. The only thing I could think about was being here and having one of the other guys, whom I barely knew, watch over me. Then there was another thought as a chill ran up my body. Nicaragua was not a very sound country, I knew there was turmoil among the people and the government. *What if something happened to Cop while he was over there? What if something really bad happened to him?*

CHAPTER ELEVEN

Cop

Everything inside me was telling me that I should never have accepted the mission in Nicaragua, but I couldn't let down my brothers. I knew that it would be dangerous. Living on the edge was the only way I knew how to survive. It was like this mission was daring me to go. Challenging everything I knew to come out on top. Sure, there was the possibility that I might not return, but the adrenaline I felt, every time I took a risk, outweighed any reason to stay. Except now there was a reason, Sabrina. I knew that I needed to survive if I ever wanted to see her beautiful face again.

We only had one more night together. Sabrina insisted that she felt well enough to go back to work. I tried to convince her to take one more day, not only to give her body time to heal, but also so that I could make arrangements to keep her safe. So when we pulled up to the gallery, I wasn't too happy to see that Hawk hadn't arrived yet. There was a lot of things that I needed to get in order if I wanted to make this a special night for Brie before I left. Escorting her inside, I scanned the gallery, out of habit, to make sure there was nothing out of the ordinary going on. I could hear some chatter in the back, letting me know that Lilly was already here. The other voice I recognized was Peter's. They were probably discussing the mission we were leaving on. By the sound of her tone, I would have to guess she wasn't pleased.

Heading to the back of the gallery with Brie walking in front just so I could watch that sexy ass of hers move, we turned the corner only to find a very disgruntled woman. Lilly's arms were crossed so tightly across her chest, I thought she was going to pull a muscle or something. Trying to alleviate some of the tension, I said, "Hey, Lilly. You're looking good."

My compliment didn't go unnoticed as Brie pulled on my arm and Peter gave me one of those "fuck off" looks. Nothing was meant by it other than to stop them from arguing. As we stood there staring at each other in silence, Brie walked up to Lilly and said, "Come on, Lilly, we need to talk."

There was no hesitation on Lilly's side as they both walked to the front of the gallery and up the steps to the second floor. Glancing over to Peter, I suggested we go back into Lilly's office so that we could also talk. Closing the door behind me, I looked over to Peter, who had settled on the leather couch. I didn't feel comfortable sitting next to him, so I stood and leaned up against Lilly's desk. Taking a deep breath, I asked, "Has there been any more news about Sean Bishop?"

Peter looked up at me like I had two horns

sticking out of my head. "We haven't heard anything. Wherever he is, he is keeping a low profile. With the police after him, I'm guessing he is hiding under an alias in some cheap motel where they don't ask any questions as long as they get paid."

"We need to find him. Peter, with us leaving on this mission tomorrow, Brie is going to more of a target for him to get his claws on her again. I know that Hawk is more than competent to take care of her, I just wish it was me," I confessed.

"Look," Peter began, "Let's worry about getting this mission done so we can get back here. You think this is easy for me? It just kills me to tell Lilly that I have to leave."

I knew that the only reason why Peter was even considering this job was because he was the only person who was familiar with the territory. I also knew no matter what I said, he was bound and determined to go.

~****~

I left Sabrina at the gallery so that I could make final arrangements before I had to leave tomorrow. The flight and living arrangements were made by Peter. Since we couldn't take the items that we needed with us, Peter got in touch with his connection in Nicaragua and had our supplies shipped over. I just hoped that we had everything we needed for the operation. I guess a government official at the American Service Embassy reached out to Peter about a month ago and explained the situation the country was in. The American officials had stumbled onto trafficking of young American woman who were either traveling alone or with another female companion. It seems the information somehow got to the traffickers from an inside source in customs when they entered the country. They were able to capture the women by posing as cab drivers sent to them by the hotel where they were scheduled to stay, only they never got there. Instead, they were taken to a remote area and held captive until they were sold to the highest bidder. The government official wasn't sure how long this was going on, but when they began receiving calls of missing loved ones, they began their own investigation.

Pulling up to the small market closest to where the cabin was, I pushed my thoughts of the mission behind me and focused on the evening ahead. More than anything I wanted this to be a night that Sabrina would never forget. Taking the few items I needed, I walked up the clerk and paid for them. As I walked back to the truck, it felt like something may have been off. I only felt this way once before; it was the day that Sarah died. Scanning the densely populated area, I searched for anything that seemed out of place. There was nothing there. Nobody that I saw seemed to pose any threat as I watched them do what normal people did. Getting in my truck I placed the small bag on the passenger seat, started the truck and headed back to my place.

The sun was beginning to set and Sabrina still hadn't made it back to the cabin. I had asked Hawk if he could bring her back to the house once she got off work. Pulling my cell from my phone I pulled up his number and waited for him to answer. "Hawk here," he said in his deep set voice.

"Hey, bro. It's getting late. Just checking to make sure everything is good," I said.

"Yeah, we're a couple of miles from your place, should be there in five," Hawk confirmed.

When I hung up with Hawk, I felt a lot better knowing that Brie was safe and with him. Placing my cell on the counter, I began preparing a meal Brie would never forget. It was my specialty. Actually, it was the only thing that I could make without burning it. It was my mother's recipe. Spaghetti with spicy meatballs in a thick sauce with mushrooms, onions, cilantro, garlic and a whole lot of other spices she put together, claiming it was her secret recipe. If I so much as whispered the contents she would ship me back to Italy in a cardboard box. My mama was always saying silly things like that. She was one-hundred percent Italian and had the ornery streak to prove it.

Just as I was finishing up, I heard Hawk's Mustang pull up the drive. The engine was so loud that I could hear it a mile away. He said it was a chick magnet and all women liked fast cars with loud engines. I told him he was dreaming.

When Sabrina walked in the house with her heels in her hand, I knew she had one of those days. I could only imagine what her feet felt like in four-inch heels all day, but then, of course a woman's body was made to withstand the torture. Grabbing them from her, I leaned over and kissed her cheek. "Rough day, huh?"

"The worst. I have never done so much rearranging and bending in my life," she confessed.

Shaking Hawk's hand, letting him know it was time to leave, I announced, "You go on upstairs and take a hot bath. I'll let you know when dinner is ready."

Brie turned and headed up the stairs while we both stared at her ass. Looking over at Hawk, I asked, "And what the fuck are you looking at?"

Putting his hands up in a surrender position, he

began backing away from me. "I got it, don't get your boxers in a bunch. I'll be back tomorrow before you leave,"

Heading back to the kitchen to check on my masterpiece, I stirred the tomato sauce a few times before I lowered the heat. Opening the fridge, I grabbed the bottle of wine I placed in there earlier to chill and popped the cork. I filled the two glasses I had set out on the counter until they were both full. Taking the filled glasses, I moved toward the stairs to check on Brie, who should have been soaking in the tub, Only when I got to the room, her body was planted head down on the bed. Somehow she did manage to take her skirt and her shirt off before she crashed. Setting the glasses down, I could hear that the bath water was still running. Careful not to wake her, I opened to door to find that the water was almost to the rim. I hurried to the faucet and turned the water off.

Brie was still on the bed and hadn't moved an inch. As much as I wanted this night to be special, I couldn't bring myself to wake her. Gathering the blanket

I had draped over the end of the bed, I gently placed it over her beautiful body and kissed her gently on the cheek. She only stirred for a moment, giving me a half smile, before she settled back to sleep.

One thing I knew for certain, once I felt she was well rested, her sweet pussy would be mine.

CHAPTER TWELVE
Sabrina

When Hawk took me home and I could smell heaven when I walked through the door, I was thankful that Cop couldn't see the ache in my heart. I had a long, exhausting day, but that was only because my emotions got the best of me. All I could think about was Cop leaving and not knowing when I would see him again. So when he suggested I take a hot bath before dinner, it was my escape. As soon as I got to the room, I headed to the bathroom to start the water. It was only when I saw one of Cop's t-shirts on the bed that I lost it. I don't even know how I managed to get my blouse and skirt off before tumbling on the bed in an emotional outpour.

I wasn't sure what time it was, the little light that had shown through the glass door had faded to darkness. The last thing I remembered was Cop covering me with a blanket and kissing me on the cheek. The only thought that ran through my mind was, *"Would he be able to taste the remnants of the salt from my tears that I shed earlier?"*

Reaching across the bed, I could feel Cop's hard body lying next to me. I pushed my sadness aside because the only thing I wanted to focus on was him and this very moment. I wanted this to be a night that he would never forget. A night that would bring him safely back to me. Gliding my hand up his bare torso, I leaned over him and began placing light, affectionate kisses up his strong body. I only stopped for a moment so that I could taste the hard disc of his nipple. His body began to stir as his hand gently forked through my long hair. He conceded to my assault by allowing me to continue my exploration to the other side of his broad chest.

His warm hands began moving down my body touching every inch of my hypertensive skin. Before I could go much further, Cop had me on my back with his perfect body straddled across mine. "Do you know how long I've been waiting to be inside you?" he asked, lowered his lips to the apex of my neck to the sensitive area just below my ear.

Pulling his body closer to mine, my pert nipples pressed against his chest, leaving me even wetter with desire. "I need you Cop, please take me," I breathed with uncontrollable desire.

Cop slowly moved his hand down my body to the juncture of my mound and slipped his hand under my lacy panties. With no warning, he removed them, by twisting the lacy material between his fingers and ripping them from my body. My desire for him erupted as he slid his hand between my legs and pushed his finger inside. My head dipped between his shoulder and his neck as he continued to shower, sweet kisses along my neck. The sensation reeling inside was like nothing I had ever felt. I never knew that I could experience such pleasure with a man. Cop made me feel desirable and beautiful, unlike the many men who took me many years before.

As he increased his movements, my body was about to give way. When his finger curled just enough to hit my sweet spot, I lost my control as my release swept through me. In a hushed whisper, he confessed, "I love when I make you come, baby."

Taking my hands into his, he placed a kiss on each knuckle, before he raised them above my head. Holding my wrists in place with one strong hand, he guided his cock inside me with the other and gently began thrusting with precise movements inside my wet channel. His hips began moving slowly as he pushed his velvety hardness inside inch by voracious inch as my walls tightened around him like a vice needing to keep him pitted deep inside.

My cry of pleasure rang when his lips parted and

captured my nipple, tugging it firmly between his teeth, sending my body spinning with complete and utter satisfaction. It was then that my gates opened and the truth came out. "Please, Cop, don't go."

The minute his lips met mine, I knew it wasn't meant to be a kiss of understanding, but a kiss goodbye.

~****~

Even though we had made love to each other on and off through the remainder of the night, my body felt unfulfilled and in need of more. Rolling over, I could see that Cop was no longer beside me and Oliver was now lying in his place. It was only after I smelled the aroma of bacon and coffee that I knew he was making breakfast. Not wanting to waste a minute without him, I hurried and put on a t-shirt and a pair of yoga pants from the guest bedroom, with Oliver following close behind. As I walked down the stairs, more of the wonderful smell entered my senses, only this time is was paired with the smell of eggs and something sweet.

When I got to the kitchen, I was disappointed to find that Hawk was standing over the stove instead of Cop. My heart began to pound, wondering where he could be at this early hour. Walking up to the counter, I poured myself a much-needed cup of coffee as I watched Hawk expertly flip the pancake browning in the pan with a flick of his wrist. Making eye contact with me, I asked, "Where's Cop? I thought he was making breakfast."

"He headed out earlier this morning. He didn't want to wake you, so he left you a note. It's over there on the table," Hawk said, turning off the burner and placing the done pancake on a plate with the others.

Hesitantly, I looked over to the table where Hawk said the note was waiting for me. Propped up against a vase holding a single red rose, I reached for the note with my name written on it in masculine handwriting. Flipping it open, I prepared myself for what I was about to read.

My Lovely Sabrina,

I am not good at goodbyes so I thought this would be the best way to tell you just that. Last night went beyond anything I have ever experienced with a woman. You have captured my heart, Sabrina; that is why this good-bye is especially hard. If I could stay with you instead of going on this mission I would, but I can't. Please don't be angry with me for leaving. Hawk assured me that he would make sure you are safe until I can return. I will come back to you. The thought of never being able to see you, is the force that will drive me back. I love you deeply, my dearest Sabrina. I only hope that you will wait for my return.

C

After I finished reading the letter, I had to read it again. My heart began breaking in two at his words. It was then that I knew, I was falling love with him. Brushing my tears away, I heard Hawk's voice. "Okay, Darlin', breakfast is served." Turning to face him, he had two plates loaded with scrambled eggs, bacon, pancakes, and fruit. I wasn't sure who he thought I was, but even at my highest appetite, there was no way I could even eat half of what he had stacked on my plate. In order not to hurt his feelings for the meal he put so much effort into, I took a seat at the table prepared to eat as much as I could of the meal. The minute the first bite entered my mouth, the bile from my stomach began to rise. Holding my month, I rose from my seat and hurried to the stairs before I could no longer hold down the contents that were ready to spill.

Reaching the bathroom, I barely got to the toilet, before the contents of my stomach emptied into the porcelain bowl. The tears, I was holding back, also began to spill. There was a light knock on the door as Hawk's voice rang on the other side. "You okay, Sabrina? I didn't think my cooking was that bad."

As I opened the door and looked up at him, I could see that he knew what was going on. Pulling me closer to him for a comforting hug, he said, "He'll be back, Brie. It will be okay, He'll be back."

~****~

The rest of my day was spent in Cop's bedroom huddled on his bed wearing a t-shirt I found in one of his drawers. I had to laugh at the band logo on the faded shirt. First Aerosmith and now Metallica. Cop must have had this shirt ever since he was a young kid. It wasn't that I had never heard of them before, it was just that I wasn't sure if they were still playing. At least for a small moment, I was able to take my mind off of Cop. That was, until I breathed in his scent as I pulled his shirt over my head, crying myself to sleep

"No, no, please don't make me go. Mommy, I promise I'll be good. I don't want to go with that man anymore. Mommy, please don't make me go." My eyes shot open at the memory of those words playing over and over in my mind. I hadn't had that dream for some time, but there it was, taking me back to the childhood that I had tucked away deep inside my head. Catching my breath, I rose from the bed, my body hot and sweaty. I knew the only reason those dreams crept back in was because of Cop. Whenever my heart felt like it was

going to burst from my chest, the nightmares were there waiting to surface like a plague needing a host to feed on. Just like the plague, my heart was slowly dying inside.

Rolling over to my side, I could see that the time was one o'clock in the morning. Pushing to a sitting position, I swung my legs over the side of the bed, careful not to wake Oliver, and slowly walked to the closed door of the bedroom making careful movements as to not stub my toe on the chair that was pushed up against the desk near the door. Reaching out my arms using them like a blind person would, I made it to the door with no injury.

The lights were still on downstairs as I went down the stairs. It made me wonder what could be keeping Hawk up at this hour. As I turned the corner to get a drink of water from the kitchen, Hawk was sitting at the kitchen table. The minute I stepped into the kitchen his head lifted and his eyes focused on mine. Pushing his chair from the table, he stood and headed my way. Reaching me, he placed his hand on my shoulder as asked, "How are you feeling, Darlin'?"

"I got thirsty," was all I could manage to say.

'Let me get you something to drink," he offered as he made his way to the fridge. As he opened the door and pulled out the water, he continued, "I heard from Cop. He and the guys landed safely. I was going to get you so that you could talk to him, but he insisted I let you rest."

"I wish you would have anyway," I said, disappointed that he didn't wake me.

"I know," he replied, handing me an open bottle of water.

"How was he? When he called," I asked.

"I think he's kicking himself in the ass for not saying goodbye to you in person. He shouldn't have left the way he did."

After our conversation, I headed back to the bedroom with my half-full bottle of water. Hawk was right. Cop should have felt bad for the way he left. Leaving a note was not the goodbye I wanted, especially not knowing how long he would be gone.

CHAPTER THIRTEEN
Sabrina

It has been a week since Cop left for Nicaragua. Even though my body is in New York, my heart is with him. The last time we had heard anything from him was a few days ago when he contacted Hawk to let him know that they wouldn't be able to communicate for a couple of days. Every day I had been trying to keep busy to keep my mind off of Cop, but it was becoming exceedingly harder with each day that he was gone. Working at the gallery and putting in a lot of hours has helped, but as soon as the day was finished, my mind found its way back to thinking about Cop and what he was doing and if he was safe.

Hawk had also tried to keep me busy. I had really gotten to know the guy that had been assigned to protect me. I hadn't heard from Sean. I was hoping that he had finally wised up and decided to leave the States. Every time I quizzed Hawk about him, he only gave me a minimal amount of information. I knew there was much more to it than not knowing where he was.

Finishing up entering the purchase invoices into the system, I headed back to Lilly's office to let her know that I was beat and was calling it a day. Over the last few days we both had been on pins and needles. Now it was just me. Peter came back to the States a few days after leaving for the mission. When I asked how Cop was, he only said that he was fine and that he was thinking about me. This made my heart sing and break at the same time, knowing that he cared and yet unable to hold him.

Gathering my things, it was late and I was ready to go home. I wasn't sure how much longer I could stay at the cabin, since it was always lonely and made me think too much about Cop. Even though Hawk was there, most of the time he was either outside scanning the area or cleaning his gun. One thing he did do a lot of, though, was cook fantastic meals.

Entering the cabin, I headed up to the bedroom while Hawk went to the kitchen to prepare our meal. I guess tuna casserole was on the menu tonight. I didn't have the heart to tell him that I wasn't really hungry, considering I had been telling him that over the past week. Just as Cop had left me, so had my appetite. It was no wonder I had the strength I did. Setting my things on the bed, I slowly undressed and went to the bathroom. Looking in the mirror, I hardly recognized myself. My eyes had dark circles under them and the lack of appetite was beginning to take a toll on my body. Even the curves that Cop had loved so much were beginning to melt away.

Standing under the spray, I tried to think good

thoughts, but the only thoughts that came to mind were of him. Closing my eyes, I began imagining him in the shower with me as his hands began gliding down my wet body. How he gently wrapped his arms around me before his soft lips took mine in a heated kiss. I could feel the hardness of his bicep muscles as I ran my hands up his arms before he cupped my ass cheeks and lifted me, pressing my body against the cool tile of the shower wall. His eager lips trailing wet kisses down my neck between my breasts, before they rested on the hard bud of my nipple. Taking hold of my breast, I imagined it was his touch against my breasts as I took the hard peak between my fingers, pinching them firmly, sending a wave of pleasure to my core. Dipping one hand lower, I parted my folds and inserted a finger inside my wet channel, picturing it was Cop pushing deep inside me.

I could only see his face as I increased my movements before I added another finger while my thumb circled my swollen clit. As my fingers filled my channel, my other fingers twisted and squeezed my nipple. I didn't know if it was the lack of sex that had my body on fire or the fact that I was thinking only of

Cop touching my body as I continued pleasuring myself. My cry of release echoed off the shower walls as my orgasm peaked, leaving me satisfied, but my heart torn and empty.

~****~

I knew that Hawk had to have sensed that something was up with me. Even though the meal looked and smelled amazing, I ended up only picking at it and taking a few bites. Taking my barely eaten food to the kitchen, I dumped it in the sink, hoping that Hawk wasn't angry that I wasted his meal. The conversation during dinner was minimal other than the customary 'How was your day' exchange that took place.

Once again, I headed to bed, while Hawk went outside to scan the area. Getting ready for bed, I noticed that Oliver didn't follow me up the steps. Heading back down, I began calling for him. I wasn't sure where he could be hiding, so as I called out for him. I searched the rooms on the main floor. When he didn't come, my only thought was that Hawk must have let him outside to go with him. Just as I reached the stairs, I had a sick feeling in my stomach. Something was wrong. Turning around slowly, the last person I expected to see was standing in front of me with Oliver in his arms.

Running up the stairs as fast as I could, I felt the pull of my ankle as a tight grip took hold. I tried to kick to get away, but it was no use. My only thought was to scream and hope that Hawk would hear me. Trying my best to get the words out, a hand came across my cheek before I could make a sound. The only thing I could hear was Oliver crying in the background. Before I knew what happened, the same hand came down on my face saying, "I told you no one would ever have you but me."

Waking up, what I thought must have been a few hours later, I tasted a hint of blood in my throat. There was a blindfold over my eyes and my hands and feet had been tied. I wasn't certain where I was, but I knew that I was in a vehicle by the way I could feel the engine vibrating under me. The floor was hard, so I had a pretty good idea that I was in the back of a van. I wasn't sure how many people were in the van. The only voice I could hear was Sean's, as he was giving another person directions to where they were taking me.

When I felt the brushing of a hand across my cheek, I knew that touch. It had been a touch that I knew all too well. That was when I was thankful that at least my mouth was free. As his finger grazed my top lip, I opened my mouth and took whatever I could take and hammered down on it. "You fucking cunt. You really shouldn't have done that," Sean said, madder than I had ever heard. It was only after his hand came down on my face in what felt like a closed fist that I knew biting him was a mistake. The pop to my face was hard enough that I no longer needed the blindfold. I was out.

CHAPTER FOURTEEN

Cop

When I talked to Hawk to check up on Brie, I never expected to hear that she wasn't doing so well. She wasn't eating and had lost at least ten pounds, according to Hawk. He also said that she was mostly running on autopilot, going to work, then coming home and remaining in the bedroom most of the night. Even the conversation was limited to 'How was your day and I'm not really hungry.' God, how I wished I was there to take care of her. I knew that it was my fault that she was sad and killing herself over my departure.

Most of my days here were filled with memories
of her. I was hurting as well. At least this mission had
kept my mind off of Brie during the day. It was the
nights that became the hardest. Lying in bed was the
worst, as I kept picturing her perfect naked body beneath
mine as I fucked her until she screamed my name. It
didn't matter that I neglected to get a picture of her that I
could carry with me before I left. Her beauty was carved
in my brain. I would never forget how beautiful she was.

One thing that was good about this mission was
that we were getting closer to the people behind the
trafficking. There was a female agent that the
government had commissioned to be on the inside who
had been purposely taken. Luckily they still hadn't
caught on to her and she was able to keep in contact
with us. Mike Chavez, one of the brothers on our team,
was also able to get inside, pretending to be a native of
Nicaragua needing a job. The government also provided
fake documents for Mike, allowing him to get inside the
operation as one of the captors. It was only a matter of

time until we would have all of them in custody. The only person we had yet to get a take on was the leader. He was very careful not to get his hands dirty in the business by steering clear of the abductions and the exchanges. We knew what he looked like and that he was still in the country. We just needed to find a way to lure him out of hiding and make himself visible.

With everything in place, all we had to do was sit and wait for another exchange. With Peter back in the States, I was left in charge and decided to take the first shift while the other men rested. We were camped out far enough away from the compound where they were holding the women that they were oblivious to our presence.

Making myself comfortable on the hill, I leaned my body against the tree and waited for any movements. The night was pretty quiet, with only a few trucks coming in to drop off supplies. I was beginning to get restless and could feel my eyes beginning to get heavy. Changing my position, I felt the vibration in my pants pocket from my cell. I had turned it to vibrate in the event Peter or Hawk called. The last thing I wanted was the blaring sound of my cell to echo down the hill to the compound below.

Pulling it from my pocket, I could see that it was Hawk calling. The only reason he would be calling is if something had happened to Brie. Normally I was the one who called him to check on things with Brie. Swiping the screen, I answered with concern. "The only reason you would be calling is to let me know something happened."

"Cop, I don't know how to break this to you, but Sean got to Sabrina," Hawk said on the other end.

"What do you mean, he got to her?" I replied confused as hell.

"I was outside scanning the area, and then that damn cat got out and I had to chase him down. By the time I got back to the cabin, Sabrina was gone. I'm not sure how he got in, but he did."

My heart sunk to the pit of my stomach. "How the hell is that even possible with all the security I have? That place is more secure than Fort Knox," I cursed.

"Yeah, well, he got in somehow and got to her. I have Peter working on information as to where he might have taken her. I'm really sorry, Cop. I never should have ran after that damn cat."

~****~

Hearing those words from Hawk that Brie had been taken, just about made me lose all control. I knew that it wasn't his fault that Sean got to Sabrina. He was no dummy. He probably had a pretty good idea how the cabin was laid out and where he could wait until he could get close to Brie.

Gritting my teeth, I said, "Fuck, I'm on the next flight home."

"Peter and I will find her. You finish what you need to up there," Hawk said.

"You can't talk me out of this, Hawk. I'm coming home."

"Cop, this mission needs you. You can't just abandon it."

"The fuck I can't."

I didn't give Hawk a chance to argue with me. After tonight, Sly was officially in change and I was out of this god-forsaken country. There was no way I was going to stay here knowing that Sabrina was in the hands of that fucking psychopath.

Morning didn't come soon enough. It was four in the morning and Lou was ready to take the next shift. Leaving him to keep watch, I needed to talk to Sly. I knew that he would still be asleep so I walked over to where he was bunked. Unzipping the door, I heard the click of his gun and his cocky voice. "One step closer motherfucker, and your face is hamburger."

"Take a chill, Sly. It's only me," I said.

Sly had the light on me in an instant as he lowered his weapon. "Jesus fucking Christ, Coppoletti, I could have shot your face off."

"Sorry," I began, kneeling in front of him. "I needed to let you know that I have to abort the mission. Shit is happening back home and I have to be there."

"Yeah, I was wondering when you were going to tell me. Peter called and let me know the scoop. Told me to convince you to finish the mission," Sly confirmed.

"You can't talk me out of this, bro. If anything happened to Brie, I would just die."

"That bad, huh?" Sly asked.

"Yeah."

"Then far be it for me to talk you into staying. I know if it was my girl, I would do the same."

Finishing our little man to man, I headed across the ridge to where we had our convoy of vehicles parked. I climbed into the one closest to the road and hightailed it out of there. Turning the key and throwing it into drive, I headed down the long road. I only loaded what I needed inside my backpack because at this point, stopping back at the hotel wasn't an option. I needed to get back to the States and fast.

Pulling up to my place, I could see that Peter's Camaro was in the drive. Grabbing my bag, I headed inside the house to get a rundown on what had transpired since I was up in the air in that piece of shit scrap metal. It was the only form of transportation I could get on such short notice. Placing my things by the door, I could hear Peter and Hawk talking in the kitchen. As I headed that way, I tried not to think about all the things that could be happening to Brie. Every second she was with that motherfucker increased the chances that he would kill her. Given the way she looked the last time he got a piece of her, her chance with him was next to null even with the little self-defense moves I showed her.

Peter and Hawk were sitting at the table looking through some documents that looked more like location maps. As my boots hit the ceramic tile, both of their heads turned. Peter shook his head before he said, "Bro, you should have stayed in Nicaragua."

"Peter, you of all people should know better than to say that. What if it was Lilly? Would you feel the same way?" I asked, knowing his answer.

"Point taken, Cop," he replied.

Taking a seat next to Hawk, I picked up the maps and questioned them both. "So what are these?"

"We found them in the sleazy hotel Sean was staying at. It looks like terrain maps of some sort. We're trying to figure out where it may be," Peter confirmed.

As I looked at the maps more closely, I recognized the area on one of the maps. "I think I might know where this is at," I said, pointing at the sight in the middle of one of the maps. "I think this is where a missile site used to be. My dad used to take me there when I was a kid."

"Do you know how to get there?" Hawk asked.

"Yeah, it's up-state, by the Adirondacks. Do you guys think he took her there?"

"I think it would be worth it for us to check it out," Peter claimed.

It was a good four-hour drive from where we were at to the Adirondacks. Even though my body was beat from lack of sleep, I knew we couldn't waste any more time. If Brie was there, we needed to get to her as soon as possible.

CHAPTER FIFTEEN

Sabrina

I wasn't sure where Sean had taken me, but the room I was left in felt cold and damp. There was also a musty, damp smell, like it could have been in a cellar. Even though I was no longer blindfolded, my eyes were having a hard time adjusting to the darkness. Adjusting my position, I managed to sit upright and eventually stand. I began scanning the room, but found that I couldn't see anything. Putting my arms out in front of me, my only option was to hopefully find a wall that I could move along until I was able to find a door or anything that would give me some small hope for an escape.

When I finally touched the cold concrete wall, I began walking along it trying to make my body cooperate. My legs felt like I had run a marathon and my right angle throbbed like it may have been sprained. I knew I must have been getting closer to the door because the temperature had changed and I could now feel a cold breeze hit my face. The air made my face feel a lot better. I could only image what a wreck it was after the fight I put up with Sean.

Feeling a gap between the wall and what I assumed was the door, I tried to find a handle. There wasn't one that I could feel, at least not where I would expect one to be. *"What kind of fucking door is this,"* I thought to myself as I continued to try to find anything that would tell whether or not this was even a door. Feeling the gap again, I lowered my body and began running my fingers in the crack, hoping to find some sort of latch. It was only when I got to the other side of the door that I felt something that could have been a way to open. It was no wonder I had missed it before. About half way down the door were two small holes in the metal that were large enough to get a finger inside.

Placing my index finger and my middle finger in the holes, I began tugging at the door. When that didn't work, I shifted my weight and tried to slide the door open. There was a little resistance, but the door finally slid open. It wasn't my strength that opened the door, but the burly man standing on the other side. I had never seen him before, so it made me wonder who the hell he was.

"Looks like the little lady has decided to wake up and honor us with her presence," he said sarcastically.

I was in no mood for his humor. "Who the fuck are you, asshole?" I asked, inching slowly away from his large frame.

"Now, now, is that any way to talk to me, princess?" he said with a cocky grin.

I didn't realize that as I inched away from him, he inched closer. My movements caused me to back right into the cement wall, trapping me in a corner. He was so close to me now that I could smell the sweat and stench of his soiled clothing. He stunk so bad, I was certain that he hadn't showered in a month. When he brushed his grimy hand along my cheek, it took everything I had not to spew all over him. I tried to turn my head away, but he stopped my movements by pinching my cheeks between his fingers.

"If you want to stay alive, you better be a good little girl," he whispered as his face was now inches from mine.

I knew he was going to plant his lips on mine. Closing my eyes as tight as I could to shut him out, my head began spinning with memories of the last time someone had forced themselves on me. Just when I thought another panic attack was going to enter, I heard a familiar voice. "Leave her alone, Ben," Sean said from behind him.

Looking down to his side, he stepped back and allowed Sean to come into full view. It was only then that I realized that it was the gun he was holding in his hand that persuaded the burly guy to step back. Putting his hands up in surrender, the man said, "Just wanted to scare her a little, boss. Didn't mean anything by it."

"Scare, my ass," I thought to myself. If Sean hadn't come in, he would have taken what he wanted without asking. Just like all the other scumbags from my past. As I got the room, I needed to breathe, Ben left the room, leaving me alone with Sean. I wasn't sure what was worse, being mauled by Ben or being alone with Sean. Gaining my confidence, I looked him in the eye and said, "You can't hold me like this, Sean. You need to let me go."

"I can't do that, Brie," he said, pacing the floor as his hand raked through his hair. "Listen, I need to keep you here."

"Why, so you can get your kicks by beating the

shit out of me?" I replied coldly.

"You needed to learn respect, Brie. If you would do as I ask instead of misbehaving, I wouldn't need to keep punishing you."

"Punishing me. Are you fucking kidding? You're a psycho!" I yelled, just before he walked over to me to backhand me across the cheek. I guess the truth hurt.

"Shut up, Brie. Unless you want me to do it for you. If you would have just listened to me and stayed away from that security guy, we could have been miles away by now sipping Tootie-fruity drinks on a beach somewhere."

"Are you even listening to yourself? I would never go anywhere with you."

"You're mine, Brie. Always have been and always will be. We are in this together. I may have made mistakes in the past that have put me in this position, but the one thing I'm sure of, I'm never going to let anyone hurt you. We're done talking. You can either come with me or stay in this room."

"Where are we going?" I asked, thinking of a way I might be able to escape this deranged man.

"Upstairs, where you will be more comfortable."

I wasn't sure where we were going, but we got into an elevator with a pull-down door. As we ascended, I kept thinking of a way to escape. If I could just catch him off guard, I would be able to use some of the maneuvers that Cop taught me. The only problem was that I couldn't get to the gun he had stuffed in the back of his pants. My chance to escape came and went as the elevator stopped and Sean lifted the heavy door. Looking around from the inside of the elevator, it was like I had stepped into a different dimension. The room was fully decorated with state-of-the-art furniture that looked like something that would have come out of a James Bond movie.

Stepping off the elevator, I took a better look at

my surroundings. Even though there were no windows that I could see, the room was very well lit. The fake windows, that I had to take a second look at, were decorated with scenic views of beaches and mountains. When the scenes began moving, I knew there must have been a projection of the pictures shining from somewhere in the room.

"Follow me and I'll take to where you can freshen up," Sean said, looking over his shoulder.

"Why are you doing this?" I asked.

"Because this is the only way that I can keep you safe. When you have finished showering, I will explain everything."

An explanation was something I really didn't care about. I only cared about finding a way out of this place. I wasn't even sure what this place was, or where. Following close behind, Sean escorted me into a large bedroom that had an attached bathroom. I only assumed it was his since the colors chosen for the décor were more masculine than feminine. The bathroom was also very masculine. Even though there was a large jetted tub, which reminded me of the one at Cop's place, I choose to take a quick shower instead. The faster I could clean up the quicker I would be able to get out of here. Stripping off my clothes, I reached over and turned the faucet to turn the shower on. As I waited for the water to get hot, I took a look at myself in the mirror. The reflection that I saw was much too familiar. There was bruising on my right cheek and my lower lip had been split. *"Why do I keep letting men get the best of me?"* I said to myself as I placed my index finger on the cut. It was a wonder I still had my looks, considering the amount of times my face had taken a beating.

The water felt good on my sore body as I stood in the large shower that could easily facilitate four people. Looking over to the shelf, I picked up a bottle of my favorite brand of shampoo. Things began running through my mind, like how much planning went into my kidnapping and how long Sean had been planning this. Another thing was, whose place was this? And where was I?

Finishing with my shower and drying off, I headed back to the bedroom to find a clean change of clothing lying on the bed. Removing my towel, I took the lacy bra and panty set and put them on. If it hadn't been my only choice in essentials I would have never picked anything so sexy. I wasn't sure what Sean had in mind, but just thinking about it made my skin crawl. I was sure he would have preferred to see me naked and forgo the sexy lingerie. I was happy to see that at least he choose a simple sundress to cover my lacy under garments.

Once I was dressed, I began searching for anything that would assist me in finding out where it was that I was being held. Opening the dresser drawers, the only thing I saw were more lacy under-things, women's clothing all in my size. This was beginning to make me very uncomfortable. Sean not only kidnapped me, he intended to keep me here for a long time. My chest began to tighten. Walking over to the closet, I reached around the corner to find a switch. Turning on the light, the feeling in my chest got even tighter as I saw the closet filled with women's clothing on one side and men's clothing on the other.

Pushing the clothing aside, I looked for anything that I could use as a weapon. There was nothing, unless I used the ridiculously high stilettos perched on the shelving between the hanging clothes. Stepping out of the closet, there before me with an unsettling grin was Sean.

"I hope you like the things that I purchased for you," he stated.

"I don't know what you are planning, Sean, but you need to let me go," I said knowing I was wasting my breath.

"Come sit on the bed with me. We need to talk."

I was hesitant to even listen to him, but there was really no where else for me to go. Taking my place at the end of the bed, I watched as Sean settled beside me. "Whatever you have to say or explain isn't going to change the fact that you have broken the law in so many ways, and when they find me, you are going to spend the rest of your days behind bars."

"If I had my choice, I would rather be found by the police than being found by the people looking for me any day. But unfortunately for you, that is never going to happen, because I won't let it." Sean began, "I've made a big mistake, Brie, that I'm never going to be able to fix."

"What are you talking about, Sean?" I asked.

"The men that are after me are ruthless bastards. Killing me and you would only be target practice for them."

"What did you do, Sean?"

Rising to his feet, he began pacing the floor. I knew whatever it was had to be bad. Very, very bad by the way he was pacing. "Just spill, Sean."

Looking down on me, he began explaining. "I

took money, Brie. Money that I shouldn't have kept. Now they are after me."

"Who?"

"Drug people," he confessed.

"Just give them their money back," I said.

"It's not that simple. For one, I don't have it anymore. Secondly, even if I did, they aren't the kind of people that will just take it back and forget it even happened.

"What did you do with the money?"

"You're looking at it," he said, lifting his hand. "This place."

I wasn't sure what to think. Not only was he in danger, he also put me in danger as well. This was not going to happen. I needed to find a way out of here, and fast. It was then that I noticed the flower vase on the small table by the door. Standing up, I walked over to the flower arrangement and did something I thought I would never do. I began playing my part as the caring girlfriend.

"Sean, did you get these for me?" I said, pulling a rose from the vase. When I looked over to him, he pushed from the bed and began walking towards me. When he was in my personal space. I clenched my teeth in disgust and placed my hand on his cheek. "We will work together to fix this."

As he lowered his lips to mine, I reached behind me, took hold of the vase, and smashed it against the side of his head before his lips touched mine. The look on his face said it all as his body crumbled to the floor. When he didn't move, I grabbed the door knob and hurried back to the living area where the elevator was.

As I got inside and pulled down the heavy door, I was glad that I didn't run into Brutus Ben. Pushing the top floor since I knew what was below, I prayed that it would take me where I would find my escape. When the elevator finally stopped, I lifted the door only to find a set of stairs leading up. Taking them two steps at a time, there was another metal door at the very top. Pushing it open, daylight hit my face, giving me a taste of freedom. The only problem was, I had no idea where I was. Scanning the area, it looked like I was being kept in some sort of shelter. The shelter, or whatever it was, was surrounded by a chain-link fence. Running to the gate, it was locked with a chain and a padlock. My heart sank, knowing I came this far only to be trapped once again. Looking for another escape, I could see that there was a small area down the fence line where the fence had pulled away from the steel post.

I pulled the fencing back as far as I could, which allowed only a small space that I could crawl through. I managed to get the front of my body through before the sharp edge snagged the hem of my dress. Careful not to rip it, I worked the fabric free and got to my feet and began running down the road that led to who knows where.

CHAPTER SIXTEEN
Sabrina

I wasn't sure how long I had been running, but
my legs could no longer move. Slowing my pace, I
stopped for a second to catch my breath and to take in
my surroundings. It seemed that I was in the middle of
nowhere. I knew that if I kept going, eventually Sean
would catch up to me and take me back to the shelter.
Picking up my pace to add more distance, I spotted
another road. Jogging to the intersection, there was a
sign about a hundred feet ahead. It looked to be a

location sign. As I got closer, I could see that it read "Manhattan, 270 miles."

There was no way that I would ever make it. My only hope was that someone would be coming along on this road that I would be able to catch a ride with. It felt like I had been walking for hours. My feet were beginning to hurt and my throat was dry. What I wouldn't give for a glass of water. *"Maybe I could rest for just a bit,"* I said to myself. Looking for a place to rest my feet, I spied a rock on the side of the road. Sitting my tired body down, I began rubbing the soreness out of my feet. As I sat there, I heard the faint sound of an engine. Standing, I looked down the road to see that a dark-colored vehicle was heading towards me. As I waved my hands like a crazy person, the vehicle pulled over to the side of the road just in front of where I was standing. While I was running up to the passenger side of the SUV, the door opened.

"Thank you so much for stopping," I said gratefully. Only I shouldn't have been so grateful.

"Get in, Sabrina," an older gentleman in his late fifties said, pointing a gun straight at me.

As I climbed in the back seat, I noticed that there was something about this man that seemed familiar. I just didn't know what.

"I'm sorry, sweetheart to have to do this to you," he said, holding a pair of handcuffs in the other hand. "Place your hands behind your back."

I did as he asked, not ready to lose my life just yet. As soon as the cuffs clicked on, I turned to face him and said, "What do you want? If it's Sean, I left him at that shelter," I confessed.

"Mr. Bishop is being dealt with. It's you I'm interested in," he said.

"What could you possibly want with me?"

"You really don't know who I am. I've been searching for you for a long time," he replied.

"How would I know who you are? I've never seen you before today."

"I'm your father, that's how."

"You've got to be kidding," I said confused.

"On the contrary. This is something that I would never kid about. Now that I found you, I'm never letting you out of my sight."

I didn't know what else to say. I was in total shock that he was claiming to be my father. The more I took in his features, the more I could see that we did share some traits. For one thing, his eyes were the same color as mine. His hair was also the same color, aside from the graying at his temples. Growing up, my mother told me my father took off when he found out she was pregnant. She refused to talk about him whenever I asked about him. She told me it was a sin to even think about him. The only father figure in my life was my mom's pimp, at least that's what she told me. That was why it was so important for me to listen to him when he sold my soul to all those men.

Taking a chance, I asked, "Why did you leave us?"

I could tell by the way he looked at me that he didn't know what I was talking about. "I never left you. Your mother took you from me, by leaving. I wanted to get married and have a family. She wanted no part of it, so she just took off."

Being raised by my mom, I could see how he might be telling the truth. I just couldn't understand why she would have chosen the life she did instead of having a family. Wanting to know more, I asked, "Did you know about her lifestyle, the one she chose instead of marrying you?"

"At the time I never knew what her choice was. All I knew was, one day she was there willing to work things out, and the next she was gone, nowhere to be found, selling herself and you."

I wasn't sure if I trusted him enough to tell him exactly what she did to me. Leaning back against the seat, I kept my secret to myself as I watched the pine trees pass by.

~****~

I must have fallen asleep during the drive because when I woke up, we were stopped in front of a jet parked on the tarmac of what I could only assume was Teterburo. As the driver exited the SUV and rounded the car to open my door, I looked over to the man that claimed to be my father and asked. "Where are you taking me?"

"A piece of paradise, sweetheart," he said.

"And where might that be?" I asked, irritated by his vague response.

"Think of it as a surprise," he urged.

The driver took hold of my handcuffed arms and pulled me from the car. The awkwardness caused my arms to be pulled in the wrong direction. "Ouch, could you pull me any harder?"

"Charles, please be careful with her," he demanded.

The driver's grip eased and I was able to get out with no problem. The only thing I wished was to have the cuffs removed. "Can you please take these off me?"

"Only if you promise to behave," he advised.

"There is no where for me to go."

"Very well," he replied, handing the small key over to the driver.

Once the cuffs were off, my hands began to get feeling into them again. As much as I wanted to escape this man, I knew it was useless. My only prayer was that Hawk was looking for me and would be able to find me.

The driver took my arm and escorted me onto the jet plane. I wasn't sure what my so-called father did for a living. The driver showed me where to sit, while I waited for my so-called father to take a seat.

As soon as we were settled, I began quizzing him about who he really was. "So are you going to tell me why you are holding me against my will?"

"I wouldn't think of it that way, sweetheart. Think of it as a father protecting his child," he said.

"You don't even know me and I certainly don't know you," I began, shifting my position so I sat a little taller.

"I know more about you than you think. I also know about your mother and the kind of life she dragged you into. No child should have to go through what you did, but I have taken care of that as well. No one will ever hurt you again, Sabrina," he advised.

"Okay, since you are claiming to be my father, I

think it is only fair that I know who you really are," I questioned.

"All you need to know about me is that I am not going to let anything happen to you."

"I don't even know what to call you," I voiced in annoyance.

"Well, I would love for you to call me Father or Dad, but I know that would be uncomfortable for you, so you may call me Lee," he said.

~****~

The flight to who knew where was taking way too long. I knew we were no longer in the States as I watched the body of water, what I assumed was the Atlantic Ocean, come into view below us. Seeing the body of water made me wonder where we were headed. The only thing Lee said was 'a piece of paradise.' It had to be some remote island somewhere where he could keep hidden. As I sat back and looked out the small window, a woman entered the area where we seated. She must have been some sort of flight attendant, because she was carrying a tray of drinks. When she walked over to me she asked in a fake voice, "Hi, my name is Beth. Would you like something to drink?"

Looking up, I said, "Water would be fine."

Handing me a bottle of water, she sauntered off to some other room. Sipping on my water, I continued to look out the window. It almost seemed like we weren't moving the way the ocean stilled. It wasn't until I saw a few islands below that I knew we were getting close to some sort of civilization. The voice of the plane's pilot came on over the intercom, announcing that he was getting ready to make his decent and to make sure we were seated with our seat belts on.

There was a small airport on the island that we landed on. It didn't look like much twenty thousand feet in the air, but the closer we got, the better I could see that it was actually a private airstrip. The view was spectacular, with the beautiful flowered trees and shrubs.

I had no idea where we were, but it was indeed a piece of paradise.

When the plane landed and we had all gotten off, there was a black SUV waiting for us on the runway. The light breeze blew my hair, but it was warm and the hint of something sweet filled the air. My guess was the flowered plants that bordered the airstrip, making a clear landing path for the pilot. The driver of the SUV stepped over to where Lee was standing and said something in a language I didn't understand. It almost sounded French, but my guess was that it was Creole. When their conversation was over, the young driver walked over to the back passenger door and held it open and waited for us to get inside. Once we were settled, he rounded the vehicle and got in himself.

As we drove away from the airstrip, I noticed that we never got on an a main road. The road we had taken was dirt and led us through a heavily wooded area of palm trees. As I took in the scenery, Lee placed his hand on my knee. When I flinched at his touch, he said "We are almost there."

"Where is there?" I asked, knowing I wouldn't be getting a straight answer.

"Your new home," he offered. "I think you will be very happy here."

I had no idea how I felt. All I wanted was to go back to New York. All I wanted was to be back in the arms of Cop. God, I hoped he was looking for me.

CHAPTER SEVENTEEN

Cop

My head was swimming with thoughts of Sabrina. I hated the feeling of not knowing what we would find once we got to the missile silo. I had to believe that we would find her and she would be okay. We decided to take Hawk's SUV only because we weren't sure what kind of terrain we would be dealing with. Turned out that most of the roads leading to the silo were very well maintained. Leave it to the government to make sure their roads were accessible. As

Hawk turned up the main road leading to the silo, I got this strange feeling in my gut that something was wrong. Approaching the fence, we could see that it was secured by a chain and padlock. Hawk didn't waste any time putting his SUV into park and walking the rear, where he pulled out a pair of bolt cutters.

In a matter of minutes the lock was off and we had full access to the entrance. Pulling through the gate, Hawk scanned the area to find a place to park his vehicle. It was only after he spotted a break in the trees that he maneuvered the SUV around them and put the truck in park. Gathering our thoughts, we decided to come up with a plan.

"So what's our move?" Hawk questioned as he looked over to Peter who was sitting in the passenger seat.

"I don't see any cameras or surveillance at the entrance. It's not to say there isn't though. I think our best bet is to wait about half an hour. When it gets dark, it's going to be our best chance to get inside, hopefully without being noticed."

I knew that Peter was right, but that half hour could make a lot of difference in what Sean had planned for her. Just as I was getting ready to argue about waiting, I saw some movement at the entrance. Crouching low in my seat, I looked over my shoulder and said, "Hey guys, door."

Peter and Hawk both looked over to where I was pointing and could see there was a guy coming out of the metal door. He was walking slower than normal, like he had been hurt or something. Needing to get a better look, I picked up my binoculars from the floor and aimed my gaze at the silo's entrance door. Focusing the lens, I recognized the body. It was Sean and he had a gouge on the side of his head that was bleeding pretty good. "God damn, motherfucker," I said with gritted teeth. "It's Sean Bishop."

"It's your call, Cop. What do you want to do?" Peter asked.

All I could see was red, I swung open the door and was out in a flash. "God dammit Cop," Peter whispered with gritted teeth.

There was no way I was going to let this guy out of my sight. Closing in on him, I could see that Sean was worse off than I thought. When he fell to the ground, I knew it was my chance to close in on him. Sean didn't so much as move as I hovered over him. Kicking him in the side, I demanded. "Where is she? What did you do with Sabrina?"

Sean barely had a chance to roll over before I planted my boot in his side. "Jesus fucking Christ, I don't know," Sean cursed, holding one arm to his side and the other on his head wound. "She hit me with a vase and took off."

I lifted his body from the ground looking at him square in the eye. "If anything has happened to her, I will personally make sure you never see daylight again."

Grabbing the collar of his shirt, I began dragging

him over to the SUV. Peter jumped out and assisted me. Once Sean was tied and we were certain there was no way for him to escape. Peter and I headed inside the silo to make sure that Sabrina was gone as Sean had said, while Hawk watched Sean. Pulling the door open, we were greeted by a round of fire. We had no idea where the gunfire was coming from. It had to be from the bottom of the stairs. There wasn't much cover that we could take. It was only when the shooter peeked his fat ass head around the corner to take another shot that Peter was able to get a shot, which landed right between his beady little eyes.

Making our way down the steps, Peter rolled the pile of shit over, only to find that his face meant nothing to him. The only other exit was a freight elevator. Getting inside, we begin pushing floors, hoping to find any sign of Sabrina. The first couple of stops ended up being only storage areas. Our guess was that was where supplies and rations were kept in the event of a disaster.

It was only after we hit our fifth stop that things began to change. It was like stepping into a different world. "What is this place?" Peter asked confused.

"I don't know, but I'm going to find out," I replied as I began scanning the living area that looked like it came out of a magazine.

With my gun drawn, I began searching every inch of this area. Who ever designed this space, must have been afraid that the world was going to end. Every room was equipped with high-end furniture and state-of-the-art electronics. If I didn't know better, I would have thought this to be the home of James Bond, Mr 007 himself.

Moving down a hallway, I could see light coming from another room. Staying close to the wall, I raised my gun in case there was someone lurking inside. Pushing the door open, the room appeared to be empty. There was broken glass surrounded by roses on the floor. I could only assume this was the vase that Sabrina hit Sean with. My chest began to feel tight knowing she wasn't here, just like Sean had stated. *"Where are you, Brie?"* I said to myself as I exited the room.

~****~

It was a long drive back into the city. Sean needed medical attention and there was still the question as to what we were going to do with him. After he told us his reason for taking Brie in the first place, we decided to hold on to him a little longer before turning him over to the police. As much as I hated the idea, I knew that he would be a great asset in finding Brie. All I could think about was where she could be. Once we left the missile silo, we looked for any signs as to where she might have gone. The only evidence we had that she escaped was the small piece of material Hawk found hanging from the fence.

Sean seemed to think that the men that were after him may have picked her up. After hearing his story, he was a bigger scumbag than I thought. If he hadn't already been beaten, I would have knocked the shit out of him for taking Brie and putting her in danger. I didn't care what his reasoning was. He had no right to inflict his money problems on her.

When Ash showed up at the cabin, he stitched Sean's head and bandaged it up. Ash had the best medical training out of all of us. He also was a great artist and was able to draw a pretty good composite of the men that were after Sean. Once he was finished with the drawings, he took them back to the shop where he could scan them into the system and hopefully get a hit on the facial recognition software we used to catch criminals.

It was getting close to night time, and Peter and Hawk were on the back deck drinking some brews. Our house guest was locked away in the basement in one of the rooms I used to use to store my training equipment. And I was punching my bag, trying to pacify some of the aggression I had. Focusing only on my fists hitting the hard leather, I didn't hear Ash come down the stairs.

"I think you've done enough damage to your punching bag for today," Ash called. "I've got some info on the sketches," he stated.

I removed my gloves and we headed up the steps to the upper deck, where Hawk and Peter were waiting. As we stepped outside, I knew whatever Ash found out wasn't good. Taking a seat, I prepared myself for the worst. "So you got some information," I said.

"Yeah, and it's not pretty," Ash advised.

"Just let me have it, Ash."

"Okay. The guys that Sean is involved with are heavy into drug dealing, among other things. Illegal arms, organ harvesting, money laundering. You name it, they're into it. The biggest is the drugs, but they aren't the main source. Ever heard of a man named Lee Draper?" Ash asked, switching his eye contact between us.

With no response he continued, "Well, he's the king with a capital K when it comes to drug dealing. The FBI has been after him for years, but have never been able to get close enough to capture him. Every time they get a tip as to where he is, he is always one step ahead of them and manages to slip through their fingers. That's not all, Cop. This Lee fellow has a daughter. The feds have been watching her for years, hoping to get a jump on this guy. It's Sabrina, Cop."

"What?" I blurted.

"Yeah, I don't think she knows. When the feds didn't get anywhere watching her, they gave up. Figured she wasn't involved with him."

"This is fucking unbelievable," I said, having heard enough.

"There's more, Cop," Ash admitted as he took a seat beside me, placing his hand on my shoulder. "Sabrina was awarded to the state when she was about fifteen. Even though most of her records were sealed because she was a minor, there were some things that weren't. I'm not sure exactly what happened to her, but it was bad enough to land her in the hospital. Her mom was involved somehow and was charged with felony child endangerment and sent upstate to a woman's correctional facility. She was sentenced to twelve years, with the possibility of parole after seven, only she never made it. Someone sliced her pretty good while she was doing her time."

"We need to find out what happened to her ten years ago. It could lead us to where she is." I didn't care what it took. I needed to know what happened to her.

"That is going to take some doing, Cop. I might have a little pull, but if it means getting my friend at the bureau in trouble, he's going to tell me where I can go," Ash confessed.

"Well then, we will just have to find another way. I will stop at nothing to find her."

CHAPTER EIGHTEEN
Sabrina

No matter how beautiful this place was, all I could think about was Cop. Even though I was allowed to go pretty much anywhere on the property, I was still being watched by Lee's guards. It has been a week since he picked me up on the side of the road. I still didn't know a thing about him aside from what he told me which wasn't much. He did seem sincere about wanting to take responsibility for his child and marry my mom. I wonder what my life would have been like if he had.

Finishing my breakfast, which consisted of fresh fruit and sweet croissant, I decided to take a walk along the beach. I had been doing that a lot since I got here. I just loved the way the white sand felt between my toes and how the warm ocean water caressed my skin as the water swept along the shore. I guess if I had a choice of being held a prisoner here or at that missile shelter, here would be where I preferred to be held captive.

As I was walking along the beach, I saw something buried in the sand. Jogging up to it, I pushed away the sand and pulled it from where it was buried. It was a small bucket in the shape of a castle top, the kind you would use to build sand castles. Kneeling down in the sand, I began scooping some of the damp sand into the bucket. It was a silly idea, but since I wasn't pressed to be anywhere in particular, I took the opportunity to have a little fun. Each bucket full of sand that I filled and carefully dumped over began to take shape. I was no way an expert in the department of castle building, but I had to admit that it was really looking pretty good. The only thing that I needed was something to use to make a bridge. Spotting a flowering bush, I walked over and pulled off some of the branches, being careful not to ruin the pretty flowers.

By the time I had finished building my sand castle, it looked like a place where someone could escape. There were ten steeples in all with a bridge made of twigs leading to the open courtyard. I scooped away enough sand and let the salt water seep in so that a small river circled the castle. I wished there would have been a way to create a drawbridge, but that would have required string to hold the twigs together so that they could be lifted high enough to block the entrance into the castle. Lost in my fairy tale thoughts, I heard a male voice coming from where the house was.

Protecting my eyes with my hand, I glance over in the direction of the voice, only to find Lee walking up to me. Before he reached me, he said, "We need to get you to safety, Sabrina."

I had no idea what he was talking about. I had no choice but to go with him the minute he grabbed my arm and pulled me to my feet. I could tell he was annoyed with my childlike behavior, because before I could protest the grip he had on my arm, he began kicking my hard work, destroying my make-believe haven.

"Do you know how long it took me to build that, asshole?" I cursed, trying to pull free.

"You will watch your mouth, young lady. I don't have time for your childish games, Sabrina," he advised.

The two guards that had been following me around like a bunch of puppies took hold of me at Lee's command. "Take her to the shelter where she will be safe."

"What's going on, Lee?" I demanded, needing to get some answers.

"Our location has been compromised. I need to make sure you are safe."

"What do you mean, 'compromised?'

"You don't need to worry about that, Sabrina. You just need to cooperate and let my men escort you to safety.

~****~

I wasn't sure how long I was in the shelter, if you could even call it that. It was more like a luxury hotel room with no windows. I tried to hear what was going on, but the walls were too thick and the door was made of metal. Sitting on the bed, I studied the room to find anything that would occupy my time. There was nothing except a flat-screen TV which hung above a fake fireplace. Once I found the remote, I pressed the 'on' button and waited for the screen to come to life. Only it wasn't a TV at all, it was a large monitor separated into six individual squares. The first square revealed the hallway just outside the door of the room I was in, and the other five were various shots of the outside of the shelter along with the beach and the main house.

Watching the monitor was certainly passing the

time away and it was also making me very sleepy. There was nothing out of the ordinary going on. I wasn't sure what the big deal was to make sure I was kept safe. My eyes were becoming heavy, so I decided to take advantage of the comfortable bed. I would close my eyes for just a minute. Maybe twenty minutes or so.

As I drifted to sleep, I kept thinking about Cop and how much I truly missed him. It was going on three weeks since he had left. All I wanted was to feel his body next to mine, pressing close to me. I wanted to feel his hands on my body, caressing my breasts while kissing me tenderly on the lips. Unable to control the thought of him, I lifted the hem of my sundress and slipped my hand inside my bikini underwear. I could feel my wetness as my finger slid between my slick folds. Imagining that Cop was the one touching me, I circled my entrance before pushing inside. My hips began moving to satisfy the piston motion I was creating with my finger. Cops beautiful face came into view as I slipped another finger inside filling my channel with the desire to have more.

Only the picture of Cop in my mind could bring me where I needed to be. Just like he would do. I placed my finger in my mouth, making sure that it was saturated with my saliva. I found my pert nipple and began circling the taut peak with my wet finger. Feeling a heated sensation, I knew that my need to release was close. I pulled my fingers from inside my channel and began circling my clit covering it with the my milky essence. As I heated with pleasure, I erupted with so much emotion that my heart ached for the man I was falling in love with.

When I was finally done with my emotional breakdown, I pushed from the bed and sauntered into the bathroom. Just as I was finishing up, I could hear the lock on the door being turned. Looking up at the monitor above the fireplace, I could see that it was one of Lee's guards standing outside the door. Having nowhere else to go, I stood where I was and waited for him to open the door.

Looking at me with confusion, he said, "Mr. Draper would like you back at the main house."

Slipping on my sandals, I followed him out of the shelter to the main house. It wasn't far to walk to the house from where the shelter was. The shelter reminded me of something you would see in Oklahoma or Kansas where tornados happened, aside from the luxury suite. *I bet they didn't have those in tornado shelters in the States.*

When we got to the house, Lee was standing in the living area looking out to the beach with a glass of liquor in his hand. The guard who escorted me to the house cleared his throat, letting Lee know we were in the room. As his gaze fell to me, Lee said, "That will be all," to the guard.

Taking a seat on the couch, I waited for him to say something. When he didn't, I decided to ask some questions of my own. "Who do you think compromised your location?"

Taking a sip of his whiskey, he said, "I have many enemies. There will be many times that I will need to protect you."

"Why exactly do you need to protect me?" I asked nervously.

"In time I will tell you, but for now, you will just need to trust me," he replied.

"I want to know now. I think I have a right to know why I am being held here against my free will," I raged.

"It would be in your best interest, Sabrina, not to ask too many questions. Now go upstairs and freshen up. Dinner will be ready in an hour."

Before I could say another word, his two book ends appeared at the doorway, ready to escort me to my room. I had never been so infuriated with a man before in my life. I didn't care that he was my father. He would never gain my trust or respect. To me, he was a two-bit hood dressed in fancy clothes with a fancy house.

CHAPTER NINETEEN

Cop

"Cop, wake up. We got a lead on where Sabrina might be," Hawk shouted, jolting me out of a deep sleep.

"Jesus Christ, what ever happened to 'Get up, Cop,' without all the yelling."

"Sorry, bro. By the way you look, it must have been pretty good," Hawk confessed.

Cop: Jagged Edge Series #2

"Fuck you."

Throwing the covers off, I headed to the bathroom to take a piss and get a shower. Hawk headed out with a chuckle, "Make sure you take care of that."

As I looked down, I knew exactly what he was referring to. My cock was so hard that the material from my boxers barely covered the head that was about ready to make its presence known. Grabbing a pillow from the bed, I tossed it in his direction and said, "Fucker."

Standing under the hot spray, my body began to relax, even though my hard-on had a mind of its own. Reaching down I took hold of my erection and gently began stroking the tight skin. The feel of my hand reminded me of Sabrina's touch. Seeing only her perfect lips wrapped so tightly around my shaft, sucking and licking while her small hand cupped the bottom of my sac, caressing it gently in her palm, I leaned my body against the tile wall as her movements increased. My hand fell to her cheek until I fished my hand in her hair. I could feel her hot breath as I pumped deeper in and out of her mouth. My orgasm was so intense that the sound of her named ricocheted off the glass walls as my release coated the glass.

As I got dressed, I started to think more about what Hawk had said. I hurried and slipped on my jeans, commando style, and headed downstairs to the kitchen to grab a much-needed cup of coffee. If I was going to hear what they had found out, I wanted to make sure I was ready and alert.

By the time I had gotten to the kitchen, the guys drank the last of the coffee, leaving me with my other choice for caffeine. Opening the fridge, I grabbed a can of Coke, popped the top and took a long sip. Looking out the glass door, I could see that Peter, Hawk, Ash, and Ryan were congregating on the back deck. No sooner had I opened the door than I had four sets of eyes looking at me like I had grown a set of horns.

"Hey, guys, what's up?" I asked, breaking the uncomfortable glares.

"Glad you could join us," Hawk said.

"So what is this about locating Sabrina?" I questioned.

"My guy at the bureau was able to find out some more information on Lee Draper. He found out that he owns several properties across the US and UK. They have already been checked out, but there is one house in the Caymans that no one has been able to get to. That was, until yesterday. Even though they weren't able to land, they were able to get a good idea as to the layout of the property. It makes perfect sense that he would be keeping Sabrina there. The property is hidden away so it's hard to see it from the air, but the landing strip is another story. This is the only way on and off the small island which leads me to believe it is where Sabrina is being held," Peter advised.

"Okay, so we might have an idea where Sabrina is being held, but how are we going to get onto the island without being noticed?" I asked.

A.L. Long

"Peter has an idea," Ash began, "Since the only way off or on the island is either by plane, boat or helicopter, we thought we could fly in as a supply aircraft. This way we would be able to land safely and leave some of the guys on the island to find Sabrina. Once she's found we would then use a helicopter to rescue her since it would be a lot faster than trying to take off."

"And how is our ride supposed to know when we needed to leave?" I asked.

"Once the plane has landed, there won't be any reason for them to think another aircraft would be in the facility. So while we are unloading the supplies, Ash is going to stay close until we let him know the coast is clear. Then he will be landing the chopper in the wooded area and wait until we are safely able to leave," Peter confirmed.

"What if this plan doesn't work?"

"It will work, Cop. We have been going over the

231

plan in great detail and have come up with alternate plans should something go wrong.

"When do we leave?"

"At 1800 hours. The darker it is when we land, the better," Peter explained.

~****~

I wasn't sure of Peter's plan. If we got caught pretending to be delivering supplies, it would mean that our lives and Brie's would be over.

Trying not to over think the plan, I looked over to Peter and asked, "I hope you're right. What about Sean?'

"I think Mr. Bishop has not proven to be an asset after all. I think our best plan is to drop him off on the steps of the NYPD and let them deal with him," he stated.

~****~

As we headed to Teterburo, I kept thinking about the plan and everything that could go wrong. For one, we had no idea what would be waiting for us once we landed. Who knew how many men were in Lee Draper's arsenal? He was a very powerful man and one that was dangerous. Secondly, we had no idea if our plan would even work. The only thing we were able to find out was the supply company's scheduled run to the island and also the name of the company. What if they began questioning the change in delivery personnel? Peter's solution was to tell them, they were called out on another run and wouldn't be back in time for the delivery. I could only pray that we could be believable enough to convince them.

As we drove up the tarmac, our plane was ready and packed full of supplies we found from a previous shipment order. Ash took the pilot position, while I co-piloted. Peter and Ryan took a seat behind us.

The control tower came over the headphones,

letting us know we were clear for take-off. Looking over at Ash I acknowledged with a nod, "Here we go."

"We should be landing in about four hours," Ash confirmed, pushing on the yoke to level out the plane at just below 30,000 feet. "Once we get to Grand Cayman a chopper will be waiting for us, but first we will refuel in Miami."

"In that case I think a little siesta is in order," Ryan confessed, pulling his ball cap over his eyes.

It always amazed me that he could catch a few Zs anywhere. It didn't matter where we were traveling or how, he always managed to sleep.

Once we hit Miami to refuel, Peter made sure to get in contact with the guys still on the mission in Nicaragua. Even though Sly was more than capable in handling the situation there, I still felt guilty leaving him with that shit storm. I was glad to hear they were ready to end the mission, even though the main guy in charge of the trafficking was no where to be found and never surfaced. The guys were able to take down ten of his guys and rescue a dozen very scared young women. Soon they would be back in New York ready to tackle another project.

One thing I wasn't glad to hear was that somehow Sean managed to escape before Josh could get him to the police station. Who would have thought the dumb fuck could slip out of his restraints like some kind of Houdini? There was no time to think about him now. Our main focus had to be on getting Brie away from that lunatic father of hers.

We were about half an hour away from the Grand Cayman where the helicopter would be waiting for us. It always seemed, with any trip, the last half hour was always the most nerve-wracking. All I knew was, I was closer to getting Brie back than I was three hours ago.

CHAPTER TWENTY

Sabrina

Sitting on the bed, I kept wondering if I was ever going to get off this island. I knew the only way off would be to jump in the ocean and swim, which was never going to happen since I never really learned how to swim, or wait for another plane to land, which was near to impossible to determine since the main house was too far away from the airstrip.

I knew that it was close to dinner and I would

need to change. According to my father, a sundress was not the appropriate attire for dinner. Walking over to the large walk-in closet, I turned on the light and contemplated the outfit I would wear. It was like walking into a fantasy world every time I stepped inside the twelve-by-ten room, which was bigger than most bedrooms. Shuffling through the clothing, I finally settled on a light blue sheath dress with three bows securing an open back. Underneath the hanging clothing was a pair of matching sling backs, with Louis Vuitton encrusted on the inside. Slipping them on, I headed to the bathroom to check my appearance before I began making my way down to the dining room. I was glad I checked; my makeup was a mess and my hair was even worse.

Grabbing my hairbrush, I began combing through the rats. I decided to go for a more demure look by pinning it up in a French roll and securing it with a emerald-stoned comb. After redoing my make-up, I was ready to make my appearance. I didn't know why I even cared about the way I looked. Lee Draper was the last man that I wanted to impress.

Getting to the bottom of the stair, I could hear Lee barking orders to his men. Something was going on. Removing my heels so I wouldn't be heard, I tiptoed down the remaining steps and slowly walked over to where the shouting was coming from. Pressing my body against the wall, I stood like a statue as I listened.

"Who authorized them to land? We aren't expecting a delivery until tomorrow," Lee said with annoyance.

"We checked their credentials, boss. Everything checked out," his guard said with confidence.

"Bring them to me, I want to see for myself," Lee demanded.

"They have already taken off. The supplies were unloaded and they left."

"Did you watch them leave?" Lee asked concerned.

"No, not personally, but the one of the other guys saw them take off."

"Get the other men together. I want every inch of this island searched. Something doesn't feel right."

I didn't know what was going on, but I knew I needed to get away from the door before I got caught eavesdropping. I only had a split second to move away before the guard saw me. Acting the innocent part, I turned and walked towards him and began cursing, "You people are unbelievable. You told me to be ready in an hour, yet none of you could be found. Do you know how long I've been looking for you guys?"

I could tell that he had no idea what I was even talking about. Continuing my masquerade I asked, "Where is he, anyway?"

"If you are referring to Mr. Draper, he is in the study," he answered confused.

"Fine," I said, walking towards the open door.

That was a little close for comfort. I took a deep breath and walked through the door. Lee was holding a tumbler of whiskey while pacing the floor frantically. Setting his glass on the end table, he walked over to where I was standing, "You look lovely this evening. Our dinner is waiting for us," he said, placing his hand on my arm in an amatory way.

Entering the dining room, the table had already been set with fine white china, crystal stemware, silverware and linen napkins. There must have been something special about tonight for the table to be so elegantly set. As Lee helped me with my chair, I couldn't help but ask, "So what is the special occasion?"

"Nothing in particular, I just thought you deserved something special after spending so much time in the shelter," he confessed.

"Shelter," I said with a laugh, "That is not what I would call a shelter. It has all the amenities of a five-star hotel, minus the view."

"That may be, but giving you this is my way of thanking you for being patient," he clarified, unfolding his napkin and placing it on his lap.

As much as I wanted to being up the conversation he had with his guy in his study, I knew I couldn't without him knowing I was listening in. So I tried a different approach to see if I could get anything out of him. "So Jack in the beanstalk seemed to be in a hurry. He nearly plowed me down."

"Jack in the beanstalk?" He questioned.

"Yeah, the guy that left your study."

"I guess one could say he has a brutish look about him. I'm not sure he would appreciate the name since he goes by Walt," he corrected.

"So…?"

"Oh... Your question. I think it's best you eat your dinner before it gets cold. Walt's behavior is nothing for you to be concerned about."

Why wasn't I surprised that he would shut down my question? Just like every other man I knew; it was a famous line. Pushing from the table, I lost my appetite. Before I could stand, I was thrown an order from his majesty.

"Sit. Sabrina, I will not tolerate childlike behavior."

His voice was so commanding it sent chills down my body. Before I could pull my chair back under me, his voice rang again. "Sit." Only this time much louder.

Unable to speak, I took my place and gathered my napkin from the table and placed it over my lap. The daggered look he was giving me was one that I never wanted to see again. Lowering my eyes, I began filling my mouth full of food that I'm sure was wonderful, but I couldn't taste. Sitting with him looking at me was worse than the silence between us. My nerves were having a heyday as my shaking hand reached for the crystal goblet filled with water and a slice of lemon. Taking a sip, I heard the weight of footsteps hitting the tile floor. Walt marched into the room with an urgency in his face.

"Sir, I'm sorry to interrupt your dinner, but we have a situation that needs your attention," he said, just low enough that I could barely hear. But I could read his lips as he began to speak.

Years of being scared had taught me one thing: always be prepared for the worst. It was then that I decided to learn how to read lips. I was certain that by his hurried entrance, it was more than a situation that needed attending.

"Excuse me, sweetheart, but there is a matter that needs my immediate attention. Walt, please take Sabrina to her room."

The last thing I wanted to do was to be taken to my room. I wanted to know exactly what was going on.

Unfortunately, I had no other option but to listen to dear old dad. Pushing from the table, I placed my napkin over my plate and proceeded to walk in front of Walt. Hearing his footsteps behind me, I knew there was no way out of this situation. I could only hope that his presence was needed to take care of the 'situation' so that I would be able to investigate what was going on once he left.

~****~

I could hear the click of the lock as soon as I entered the room. I should have known that my escape was going to be close to impossible. Changing my clothes as quickly as I could, I put on a pair of jeans and a tank top. Rushing to the bathroom, I tried to find anything that I could use to remove the screws holding the knob on. I found a small barrette that would work, but only if the screws weren't too tight. Next I needed something long that would allow me to turn the latch to the lock. The only item that might work was an eyelash curler that I requested when the first shipment of supplies came in. I only hoped it was strong enough to turn the latch. Placing my ear against the door jam, I tried to listen for any noise that may have been on the other side. When I didn't hear anything, I lowered my body to a kneeling position and began working on the screws. With the doorknob off, I slipped the latch between the curler and clamped down on the metal. Whoever said, watching reruns of Macgyver was a waste of time because none of that stuff he did ever worked, was a fool. I pulled on the latch and the door swung open.

Peeking my head out, there was no one in sight, which meant I could at least get to the stairs. Padding my way down the hall, I listened for any voices. When I didn't hear any, I looked over the staircase railing to see if anyone was wondering below. Looked to be all clear. Tiptoeing down the steps, I kept a look out for any of Lee's men. *"Something really must have them occupied,"* I thought to myself has I continued down the stairs. I knew the best way out of the house was through the back door. I crept slowly against the wall, careful not to make a sound. Turning my body to the foyer, I began walking backwards, checking my surroundings. Just as I was about to turn back around, a large hand clasped around my mouth. I had been caught.

CHAPTER TWENTY-ONE

Cop

When Peter volunteered to cause a distraction, while I slipped into the house, I never thought that Brie would be standing right in front of me. I didn't want her to give away our position, so I had to cover her mouth with my hand.

Feeling her body squirm, I needed to calm her uneasiness. Leaning over I softly whispered, "It's me, baby."

As she turned to face me, I could see the beginning of her tears start to fall. It broke my heart the minute the first one fell. Wiping her cheek with my hand, I lowered my head and took her lips and gave her a tender kiss. Her soft moans vibrated on my lips as she pulled me closer. More than anything I wanted to take her right there, but I knew we didn't have much time before Lee's men would be coming back.

Breaking the kiss I whispered, "We need to go, Brie."

Looking up at me she said, "I missed you, Cop. I thought about you everyday. I knew you would find me."

Giving her one last kiss, we headed down the hallway to the back door where I entered. Keeping her close behind me, I scanned the area to make sure I was ready for any surprises. Just when I thought we were in the clear, one of Lee's men came crashing through the door, catching us off guard. He pulled his weapon, but

A.L. Long

he wasn't quick enough. I fired a round, which hit him in his chest. His body hit the floor with a thud. I knew that we needed to get out of there quick before we got caught. Holding on to Brie's hand, we headed out the back door and down the stone path. Our efforts were once again stopped, as two more men spotted us and began firing their weapons. Firing back, I kept Brie behind me as I ran for cover. Keeping our bodies low, we ran towards a small stone ledge separating the estate property from the beach. It wasn't much protection, but it kept us from being out in the open.

Leaning our bodies against the stone wall, I reloaded my gun with the last clip I had on me. Looking over to Brie, I could see the terror in her eyes as the ringing of gunfire sounded just above our heads. Giving her hand a gentle squeeze, I asked with concern, "You okay, baby?"

Brie nodded with a small "Yes," before she looked away.

"We're going to get out of this. The guys knew I

249

went to the house and I'm sure they heard the gunfire," I assured her.

Focusing only on her, I lifted her hand to my mouth and gave it a tender kiss. Peeking my head over the edge of the stone wall, the two men who were shooting at us were laying face down on the grass. My only conclusion was that one of the other guys must have taken them out. Seeing that the coast was clear. I helped Brie to her feet and began making my way up the wall with her close behind. Still on guard, we kept our bodies in a lower position as we made our way across the grass to the road leading to the airstrip. Once we reached the road, I breathed in a sigh of relief that we had escaped getting a bullet in us. I had spoken too soon, because three more men appeared, firing right at us. A couple of times I could feel the air move next to my head as the bullet barely missed me. We needed to find cover. Taking a chance. I pulled Brie to my side and head to the wooded area on the side of the road. My only hope was there wasn't anyone waiting for us. Reaching the cluster of palm trees, I felt a sting to my left side. I knew that I needed to keep moving if I was going to get

Brie to safety.

Running through the brush and trees, I could feel my body begin to shut down, but knew I needed to keep going. I could no longer hear the gunfire as we approached a clearing. The airstrip was up ahead. Holding on to Brie's hand as tight as I could, we ran towards the other side of the hanger where I knew the helicopter would be waiting. Peter and Ash were approaching me from the other side. All I could think about was how glad I was to see them.

Meeting them by the hanger, Peter said with a drawn look, "The chopper is ready to go. I'm not sure how many men are still on this island, but we took out at least half a dozen,"

As I looked to Peter, he knew right away something was off. His eyes scanned my body, stopping at my left side where the blood was beginning to seep through my light ammunition vest. Nodding my head, I signaled him to keep quiet. The last thing I needed was for Brie to go into hysterics because I had been shot. I knew that it would be a matter of time before my blood loss would render me unconscious. The only obstacle now was getting to the chopper without getting shot. Trying to contain the pain in my side, I followed Peter, than Ash in the direction of the waiting helicopter. I made sure that Brie was in front of me as well. It was the only way that I could think of to keep her from seeing the blood stain, that was now twice the size it had been, seeping through my vest.

When the helicopter was in sight, I thanked God that we were finally able to leave this place. Ash had slowed his pace and dropped back to where I was struggling to even walk. Taking my arm, he wrapped it around his shoulder, giving me the added support to make it the rest of the way. I knew I was close to passing out as the blurred vision and dizziness began to set in. I knew that I needed to use all the strength I had to make it the hundred feet to the helicopter. Murphy's law took hold as Brie's alleged father stepped out from behind a large tree. Had Brie been a little closer to me, I would have been able to stop him when his arm wrapped around her shoulder, pinning her body next to his.

Getting to him wouldn't have been a problem either other than the gun he had pushed into her side.

"One step closer and it will be the last you see of your precious fuck thing," he began as I looked at him in confusion. "What, Mr. Coppoletti, you didn't think I knew about your little indulgence? Always one step ahead. Being in the security business, you're getting a little sloppy. You should have been more attentive. Every room of your little fuck pad has been equipped with top-of-the-line cameras. It's amazing how tiny those things are these day."

Just as I was ready to charge for him, Ash pulled me back, reminding me that at that moment Lee had the upper hand. "You fucking bastard. You would actually kill your own daughter," I said with gritted teeth as Ash held me back. I wasn't sure where my strength came from, but seeing Brie like that made me want to rip his heart out and jam it down his throat.

"Here's the thing. It's amazing what money can buy. A couple of procedures, a little persuasion, and you can get anything you want. I'm no more her father than Boy George would ever become president." he said with a chuckle. "Her real father died years ago. He should never have crossed me. Him and that slutty girlfriend of his."

"What do you want, Draper?" I seethed, barely holding back my intolerance for this man.

"I want the two million dollars that was taken from me. You get that and you can have your precious fuck thing back."

"Take this, you motherfucker," Hawk cursed, stepping behind Lee and hitting him with the butt of his assault rifle.

When Lee fell to the ground and the gun dropped out of his hand, Brie ran to me with her arms open. Leave it to Hawk to save the day. Taking her in my arms, I pressed my lips to hers for a moment before my short-lived adrenaline left and my body collapsed.

CHAPTER TWENTY-TWO
Sabrina

I knew there was something going on with Cop the minute Ash fell behind us and assisted him. I just didn't know what. When he collapsed, I saw the reason for his behavior. There was a large blood stain on his vest. He had been shot. My heart felt like someone took a hammer to it.

Ash was able to pull him from the ground with the assistance of Hawk. As they loaded him in the helicopter, I scrambled to get in myself. Taking a seat next to where they had laid him, I took hold of his hand and prayed that he would be okay, But the gray pale color of his face said it all. He was dying.

"We need to hurry, Peter," I yelled, thinking Cop wouldn't be able to hold on much longer. "We can't let him die."

"Don't worry, Sabrina, We'll get there. Hawk radioed for assistance and the medics are on standby. He's a strong man," Peter said, taking hold of my hand and giving it a tender squeeze.

The tears began to fall as I watched Cop get even more pale. He had to hold on. I hadn't even told him that I loved him. Leaning over, I kissed his forehead and whispered, "Don't leave me, Cop, I love you so much, please don't leave me."

As the helicopter rotors sounded, my heart beat kept time with each swish of the blades. Every second of every minute, I felt my heart bleed for this man.

~****~

The chopper landed on the heli-pad forty-five minutes later, and just like Hawk said, the medics were ready. As they gently put Cop's frail body on the gurney, a shallow groan escaped, giving me the hope I needed that he would be okay. As they wheeled him through the double doors, I could hear them, "We need to get him to Emergency One. Stat."

My heart began to race. All I wanted to do was crawl inside him and take away everything he was feeling. The pain, the despair, the confusion. Everything that I was feeling at this very moment I felt for him. Wheeling him in the elevator, I was stopped abruptly before I was able to join them before being told, "You will need to wait for the next ride, miss. We need all the room we can have in case we need to take action."

"Take action, what does that even mean?" I asked, confused.

"Ma'am. Please, we need to get him to surgery ASAP," the medic stated.

Before I could ask where they were taking him, the doors shut. I contemplated just running down the stairs to get to him, but I knew that it would be quicker to be patient and wait for the next elevator to arrive. I pushed the down button and waited. In the meantime, Hawk and Peter came up behind me.

"He's in good hands, Sabrina. He is a survivor," Hawk assured me as he gave me a comforting hug.

Looking at the guys, I noticed that Ash wasn't around. "Where's Ash? He should be here," I queried.

"He will be as soon as he can. The hospital CEO of Operations advised us that the helicopter had to be moved," Peter said.

As soon as the elevator door opened we were all inside within seconds. As we descended, I stared at the LED display as each floor past by. I hoped that we would be able to find where they took Cop. All I knew was Emergency One. The elevator stopped on the lobby floor, and we all rushed to the administration desk to see if they had any information on Cop.

"We were told that Cop... Excuse me, Vince Coppoletti, was taken to Emergency One. Can you tell us where that may be?" Peter asked in a calm voice.

The volunteer at the desk began typing on the computer to pull up any information she had. "You are correct, sir. He is on the fourth floor. You won't be able to enter the restricted area, but there is a waiting room there that is quite comfortable where you can wait."

Peter thanked the volunteer as we all headed in the direction of the elevator that we just exited. As we stepped inside the open door, my chest once again began to tighten. Taking a deep breath in and letting it out, I used the technique that my psychologist had taught me so many years ago. I hung back as Peter and Hawk exited the elevator. My chest was so tight, I could hardly breathe. Both of them looked at me with concern.

"Sabrina, are you okay?" I could hear Hawk's voice, even though I couldn't respond.

"Sabrina," he said, reaching out to me.

It was only after he took me in his arms that I acknowledged his presence. "I just need a minute," I said softly.

"Take all the time you need, sweetheart," he said, still comforting me.

I held him close like he was some sort of security blanket. He was the best comfort I had. I only wished it was Cop holding me instead of fighting for his life. Pushing from the elevator wall, I exited the elevator with Hawk holding on to my hand. Moments later we were at the restricted doors, where yet another volunteer sat behind a small desk.

As we approached her, it was Hawk, who said, "We are here for Vince Coppoletti. He was just brought in."

Once again, she entered the information on the screen and waited for it to load. "Yes, I see that he is still in surgery. If you would like, you may take a seat in the waiting area. I will let the attending physician know that he has family inquiring about his condition."

Walking to the waiting area was telltale of how I felt. It was an agonizing pain not knowing what was going on with Cop. Waiting rooms were like the before and after just waiting to crash down on you. As we sat, my anxiety got the best of me. I couldn't just sit and wait for the news that he was gone forever. Standing, I paced the hard linoleum floor. It was a good thing that they were covered in layers and layers of wax because the way I was pacing, there would be nothing left of the shine on the sterile floor.

Peter walked up to me, taking me away from my thoughts as he grabbed my hand. "Brie, you are going to kill yourself with worry. It isn't helping you or Cop. Trust me, he is in good hands."

"I'm so scared for him, Peter. What if he doesn't make it? I never even told him how I felt about him," I choked.

"He knows, believe me, he knows. That's why, if for any reason, he is in there fighting for you," Peter confirmed.

Walking me back to where Hawk was sitting so calmly, I took a seat, took in a deep breath and waited for the inevitable. The quietness was killing me. *"How could they be looking at the* Sports Illustrated *Swimsuit Edition, while Cop was fighting for his life?"* I thought to myself. I would never believe that they could be that shallow, looking at half-naked women. Maybe it was their way of dealing with this shit storm. I couldn't even image how hard this was on them. I knew they were close and that they all served together. That is a bond that can never be broken. While I was lost in my thoughts, Ash walked into the room with a concerned look on his face.

"What's the news?" he said as he approached us.

"No news, bro," Peter said, pulling his eyes from the magazine.

"Well, if I know Cop, he'll pull through," Ash asserted.

"How can you guys be so calm? Don't you get it, he could die?" I screamed, walking away from them.

"Brie, stop!" Peter yelled from behind me. "Cop has been through a lot worse, believe me. He will pull through this with flying colors."

~****~

Every minute that passed seemed like hours. I was becoming antsy not knowing what was going on. It was taking too long. When we hit the sixth hour, I was just about to protest by going up to the volunteer and demanding some news when a man in scrubs walked through the restricted doors. As he approached Peter,

Hawk, and Ash, I hurried and took my place right beside them.

"The surgery went well. Mr. Coppoletti lost a lot of blood, but he is stable for now. We were able to remove the bullet and the small fragments from his abdomen. He isn't out of the woods, but we expect a full recovery. He was fighting for his life in there," the surgeon informed us.

"Can we see him?' I asked.

"Mr. Coppoletti is highly sedated. He won't be alert for a couple of days. Give him time to heal. You can see him one at a time. I will let you know when he has been moved to ICU," he stated.

Looking over at me, Peter nodded as I stepped forward. "I would like to see him, if I could," I acknowledged.

"I will send a nurse when he is settled. He will pull through this, I assure you."

With those last words, the tension in my body began to subside. It was like a weight had been lifted. Even though Cop was sedated, I needed to let him know everything. I loved this man with my whole heart and he deserved the truth.

It wasn't long that until the nurse came and led me to Cop's room. He was hooked up to so many machines. I was thankful that the majority of them were to monitor his vital signs. As I walked to his bed, I could see that his face had more color to it than when he was in the helicopter. He was naked from the waist up, covered with a bandage that wrapped around his defined abs. I could see his chest rise and fall, which gave me comfort. Pulling a chair beside the bed, I took hold of his hand and began my confession.

"I don't even know where to begin. I hope that you can somehow hear me. I love you so much, Cop, that my heart hurts seeing you like this. I love you so much that I need to share with you something that I have not shared with anyone since I was fifteen years old. My childhood had been less than perfect. Down right pathetic is more like it. My mother was not a very good person. She did things that were unfathomable. For two years, she let men do what they wanted to me. I only wanted my mom's love. That was until, the last man got the best of me. I had had enough, only he didn't see it that way. He was psychotic and he took everything from me. He got so angry that he pulled a knife on me and sliced me from my navel to my side. He thought that he left me for dead. I wish I died that day, because even though he didn't kill me, he took one thing: I will never be able to have children. I lost my mom that day too. They took her from me and placed me in the custody of the state, where I lived in foster home after foster home until I turned eighteen. Since then, I have never spoken to her or seen her. I never want to go back to that, but it seems that I could never get away from that type of abuse. Until I met you."

CHAPTER TWENTY-THREE

Cop

I must have died and gone to heaven because the voice I was hearing was that of an angel. I could hear her, but I couldn't see her. It didn't matter how hard I tried, her beautiful face wouldn't come into view. Maybe I had died and it was a voice from below sounding in my head. I wish I could reach out to her. I could feel so much pain in her words. I could feel the pain she was feeling. The torment of not being able to forget something that happened so long ago. And then when she said she loved me, I knew it had to be an angel from above. *Why can't I reach for her? All I want to do was pull her in and hold her. Comfort her. Why can't I see her face?*

It is silent now. All I can hear is the faint sound of a continual beep, beep, beep. Is it the bell calling me to heaven's gate? Letting me know it's time to enter? I'm not ready to go. I need to see the angel first. *Why is it so hard to open my eyes? I can see clearly, but I can't see her. Wait, what is that? I hear her voice now. She sounds scared.*

"What's wrong with him? God, someone please help him!" she is shouting frantically as I listen.

"Miss, you need to back away so we can help him," another voice said. "Bring in the crash cart stat."

"What is going on? Why can't I move? Jesus Christ, that hurt. What the hell was that?" I shouted, hoping someone would hear. God, there's that pain again. It feels like a lightning rod going through me.

Holy Mother of God, am I being punished? There's those voices again.

"He's back. Good work, team."

As annoying as it was, it was also somehow comforting to hear it, *beep, beep, beep.* I wonder what just happened. I feel different. I feel relaxed and very tired. Maybe I can rest for a bit. Close my eyes for just a minute.

My angel was back. I could hear her beautiful voice. "Don't ever scare me like that again, Cop. You fight for us, do you hear me?" she said.

"I will fight for us. Even though I can't see, somehow I love you too," I shout with no sound coming out.

It's silent again. I hate the silence.

~****~

God, my body hurts, I feel like I have just been run over by a truck. Finally, I feel like I can open my eyes. God, they hurt too. Opening my eyes slowly, I tried to gain focus on my surroundings. Finally able to open them, I can see that I am in the hospital. There are all kinds of wires hooked up to me. My side hurts like hell, but I get to see what was going on with it. Something has me pinned down. Turning my head to the side, I see Brie's beautiful face laying across my arm. God, she looks so beautiful. She also looks like she's hurting. It was then that I remember hearing her voice. I thought it may have been an angel, but it was her. She was the one who lived through so much pain.

With my other hand, I gently move the hair from her face, rubbing my finger softly across her cheek. Her head rose as her beautiful brown eyes meet mine.

"Cop, oh my God, you're awake," she said with excitement, pressing her lips to mine.

"So, I guess it is really true. You do love me," I whispered between breaths.

"You heard what I said?" she asked.

"Every word. At least I think I did."

"So you know about my past. My mom, the men."

"Yeah, pretty much."

My heart just about died when the tears began falling down her beautiful face. I wasn't sure if they were tears of happiness or sadness. All I knew was that I loved this woman more than life itself. I think she was the main reason I fought so hard. With my free hand, I began stroking her hair, hoping that I would be able to comfort her.

"I thought I lost you, Cop. Your heart stopped beating. The doctors had to bring you back. I was so scared," she confessed.

"I heard your voice, Brie. The sweet angelic

voice brought me back. I didn't want to be without you." I replied, true to my own confession.

Once her head lifted, her eyes focused on mine. Sweeping her cheek with the back of my hand, I leaned closer and kissed her soft, tender lips. Her whimpers of her love rang through and my body began to come alive. If I wasn't in this hospital with all eyes peeled to us, I would have taken her right then and there. Not only was my body coming to life, so was my cock as our kiss deepened.

"We better stop, baby, otherwise I won't be able to contain myself, and you wouldn't want me to show you how much with all those eyes upon us."

Brie let out a small giggle as her face lit up with joy, probably contemplating doing just that. Her thoughts were put on hold, as a nurse walked in.

"Mr. Coppoletti, it's so nice to see you awake. You gave us quite a scare," she said sympathetically.

"Never a dull moment," I replied, shedding a little light on a difficult situation.

"Never is, Mr. Coppoletti," the nurse replied.

When the nurse left, satisfied with my vital signs, she informed me that I would be moved out of ICU into a private room. That was the best news yet. I knew that soon I would be on my feet and ready to travel back to the States. Everything that happened on that miserable island was the cause of one man. Well, technically two, if you include Sean Bishop. Just thinking about it made me remember that there were some things that Brie didn't know about her mom. Like the fact that she was dead. I needed to tell her the truth. She had shared so much with me about her past, the last thing that I wanted to do was to keep things from her.

Eight hours later, I was wheeled into a private room. It was no better than the room in ICU, but at least it was private and nobody would be watching my every move from a monitor. A nurse came in every thirty minutes to check my vitals. There was a lot that could be done in thirty minutes with Brie, especially since I was doing everything I could to contain myself.

Brie knew how much I hated hospital food, just by the way I pushed it away when the orderly delivered it. Feeling sorry for me and wanting to make sure I kept up my strength, she went to a local cafe to see what she could find. While I waited for her to return, Peter, Hawk, and Ash showed up. It was so nice seeing the guys. I couldn't remember a whole lot after Lee had Brie at gunpoint. I needed to know that he was either dead or in custody.

"Hey, guys," I began as I pushed to a sitting position. "Fill me in on what happened. It's a total blur after Lee managed to get his hands on Brie."

"We got him, Cop. We turned him over to the Cayman police. He is going to be extradited back to the States, where he is going to be facing multiple federal charges. He's going to be given a permanent home behind bars," Peter confirmed.

"How about the other scumbag? Any word on Sean?" I asked.

"Not yet. You leave finding him to us. All you need to worry about is getting better. You've got a beautiful woman that has never left your side, waiting to share a life with you," Hawk chimed in.

"Did I hear someone say beautiful woman?" I heard as Brie walked into the room carrying a bag full of food.

As I ate, Brie, Peter, Hawk, and Ash continued talking, letting me know what actually happened on that small island. I could only imagine how scared Brie must have been. To be held, not knowing if you would ever be set free or able to escape. I knew one thing for certain, when I got out of here, I was never going to let my beautiful Brie out of my sight.

~****~

The day finally came. The doctors finally agreed

that I was strong enough to travel. Three days in the hospital was long enough. There was still no word on Sean Bishop, and that in itself made me want to get back to the States as soon as possible so that I could begin working on finding him. With him still walking the streets, Brie was in more danger than ever. I had no idea what Sean's agenda was with Brie, but one thing for sure: I was not going to wait to find out.

One thing I was thankful for was that we were actually flying in a commercial plane, verses the cargo plane we came in. First class was everything and more. Even though I wasn't able to have the beer that I so wanted, the service was beyond impeccable. It was a long trip back, so it didn't surprise me that Brie fell asleep resting her head on my shoulder. Everything about this moment was perfect. It didn't even matter that my side was killing me. Peter must have seen my discomfort, because he stood and reached inside the overhead compartment. Pulling down my small duffel bag, he unzipped it and found the prescription the doctor left me back in Grand Cayman. Popping the lid, he shook two of the white pills in his hand and handed them to me.

The flight was so smooth that our four-hour flight went by faster than I thought. When the pilot announced our final descent, I touched Brie's cheek, letting her know that we were going to be landing soon. Her eyes were sleepy, but beautiful. More beautiful than ever only because I knew the love she had for me. One day I was going to make her mine permanently.

CHAPTER TWENTY-FOUR

Sabrina

My heart was filled with joy the moment Cop opened his eyes. When the doctors came into the room after the monitor started to flat line, I thought for sure that I had lost him. He really did have the will to fight. It was the scariest thing that I had ever gone through.

As we were heading home, all I could think about was how life would be spending it with Cop. I wondered if he would ever consider leaving Jagged Edge Security and leading a more simple life. Maybe he could be a contractor. I knew how talented he was with a hammer and nail. This was something that I really wished he would do. Him being in danger all the time was beginning to take a toll on me. I don't think my heart could take another blow like it had over the past few days.

I could hear the pilot's voice come over the intercom saying that we were making our final descent. I didn't want to move. I felt so comfortable and secure leaning against Cop that I never wanted to leave this position, but when his soft hand touched my cheek, I couldn't help but smile.

Pushing away from him. I looked out the little porthole window to see that the lights of New York were below me. It was comforting to see the brilliant lights of my home gleaming in the night.

"Ladies and gentlemen, we are about ten minutes away from JFK. Please make sure your trays are in their upright position and your seat belts are fastened securely," a flight attendant announced over the intercom.

I had never been so happy to be home. As I heard the landing gear engage, my heart began to flutter with excitement. It was only after we landed that I knew everything from this point on was going to be different. This was going to be a new beginning for both of us.

~****~

Now I knew why I hated to fly. It wasn't the flying part I hated, it was getting off the plane and dealing with the swarm of frequent flyers and their restless children that was less than desirable. I thought we were never going to get out of the airport as we waited for what seemed like eternity for our luggage.

When we stepped outside the airport, I was glad to see that Sly was leaning up against a black Excursion. Helping with the little luggage we had, Peter got in the front, while the rest of us climbed in the passenger seats. When the coast was clear, Ash pulled away from the curb and proceeded to take us home.

I was so glad to see the large cabin come into view. Peter helped with the two bags we had and said his goodbye. He confirmed that he would be back in the morning to check in on Cop. I was so glad that Cop had so many good friends. I wasn't sure exactly what kind of bond these guys had, but I knew they all had served together. To have friends like that was very rare. Growing up, I never had that.

As we entered Cop's home, we walked up the steps where I assisted him in removing his clothing and getting into bed. The large bandage on his side was a reminder how he almost lost his life. Once he was settled, I covered him with just a sheet and turned to get ready for bed.

"Where are you going, Brie?" he asked with confusion.

"To the other room," I said.

"Oh, no you're not. After everything we've been

through, I am not letting you out of my sight. Now get over here," he demanded.

"Cop, you need your rest. If I get into bed with you, I know you won't be doing much of that."

"I don't care. Brie, this is not up for discussion."

How could I refuse him looking the way he did? Removing my jeans, I slipped in beside him and nuzzled up to his side. God, it felt so good to have him holding me in his arms again. "Tell me if I'm hurting you, Cop," I whispered, cuddling even closer to him.

"You could never hurt me, Brie. Matter of fact...."

There was no way I was prepared for what he did next. Before I could protest, my body was under his. "Cop, your side," I said concerned.

"Fuck my side, Brie. All I want is you," he announced.

His lips were on mine before I could say another word. With the way they felt, I couldn't say anything even if I wanted to. Pulling me closer, he began working the t-shirt I had on over my head. Breaking for a moment, he slid it over my head and resumed his position above me, kissing and twirling his tongue with mine. This was the heaven that I wanted more than anything. He was my heaven. Cop's hands caressed my body, releasing the front clasp of my bra. My arms fell as he lowered the straps, leaving my breasts fully exposed. "God, do you know how much I've wanted these babies?" he commented, taking my hard nipple into his mouth, teasing and sucking it, bringing the wetness between my legs to an overflowing pool of ecstasy.

Lowering his hands further, he twisted his finger between my skin and my panties, causing just enough pull that the lacy material tore apart, giving him full view of my body. "You are so damn beautiful, baby," he said between breaths.

"Please, Cop. Take me, don't let me wait any longer," I pleaded.

His hand moved up my inner thigh as his other one moved to hold my hands in place above my head. His touch was so soft and tender that it was driving me crazy. Each barely there kiss sent a pulsation to my core. I knew I was going to come before I even got a taste of him. He was driving me crazy with his tenderness. All I wanted was for him to take me hard and never stop. It was only after his finger entered me that my body went on pleasure overload. Every inch of my being was on fire for this man. "I'm going to consume every inch of you, baby, and when I'm done, I'm going to start all over again," his words rang and my body exploded.

Just when I thought my pleasure could go no higher, Cop removed his gym shorts and entered me inch by inch. The feel of his cock pushing inside me was like nothing I had ever felt before. My walls squeezed him, trying to pull him deeper inside. I was lost in the sensation of finally being free. Free of the demons that had held me prisoner for so long. Free to love again, something I thought I would never have.

Holding onto Cop with everything I had, my release thundered inside me, sending me in a free fall to a place only known as Heaven. Cop continued thrusting inside me, giving me that extra sensation, building me, taking me once more to the land of ecstasy before my body once again spiraled out of control into complete bliss. His nirvana soon arrived, sending his body to join mine.

Unable to sleep any longer as the sun peeked through the blinds, only thinking about my night with Cop, I wanted to do something special for him. Slowly pushing from the bed, I walked quietly out of the bedroom and down the hall to the guest room, where most of my things still were. Slipping on a clean t-shirt, underwear, and a pair of shorts, I headed down the steps to make Cop the most amazing breakfast he would ever have. When I opened the fridge, I could see that it was pretty empty. With everything going on, I guess the last thing anyone was thinking about was food. Pulling out the only ingredients worth using, I opened the carton of eggs to make sure they were still good. Satisfied that they were still safe, I placed them to the side and began opening the cupboards to see what else I could conjure up.

By the time I had hunted through every cupboard and every drawer, I had what I needed to make a decent breakfast. The only thing that I didn't have was orange juice, but coffee was better than nothing. Humming away while I cooked, which I did often, I didn't hear Cop coming up behind me. He scared the crap out of me when he wrapped his arms around my waist.

"Geezers, Cop, you scared the begeebers out of me," I said, almost smacking him.

"Sorry, babe," he began to laugh, "I didn't mean to."

"It's not funny, Cop."

Kissing me on the cheek, he said genuinely, "I'm sorry, but the look on your face…"

"I know, priceless."

As I turned to face him, the bandage covering his gunshot wound was drenched in blood. "Cop, your side," I said frantically as I began grabbing anything that could help soak up some of the blood.

"It's okay, Brie," he said calmly. "I'll go upstairs and change the dressing."

"Let me go with you. I can change it better than you."

As we headed up the stairs there was still a small mischievous grin on Cop's face. I wasn't sure what he was thinking, but he was up to something. Entering the bathroom, I ordered him to sit on the toilet while I got the clean bandages ready. It felt good to be in command for a while. Only that while didn't last long as he pulled me onto his lap and began kissing the area behind my ear that he knew drove me crazy with pleasure. "Cop, I need to get this bandage changed," I moaned at the touch of his lips on my skin triggered my arousal.

"But I want you, Brie," he protested.

That was all it took. I wanted him too. Lifting my body from his, I pulled down my panties, threw them to the floor and straddled his lap. I could feel the arousal hidden beneath his shorts. Still straddling his legs, I stood long enough to pull his shorts down, exposing his healthy cock waiting to be consumed by me. Adjusting my position, I gently took hold and began easing my body down on his. The size of his cock was massive and all I wanted was to crash down on him, feel every inch of his girth inside me, only I knew I needed to take it slow in order to accommodate him. Moving my hips up and down in slow even movements, my channel began opening for him. It took everything I had to control the hunger I had for him. I was already on the edge of explosion, but knew that I needed to wait for him. As his hands took hold of my hips, he lifted my body from his, bending me over the bathroom counter. The emptiness I felt without him inside soon left as he slowly began driving his impressive shaft inside me, filling me with pure ecstasy.

Taking me this way was unlike anything I had ever experienced.. He was in total control. His hands left my hips, only to be repositioned on my clit and lower back. It wasn't until his hand dipped between my cheeks that my body began to tense. "You need to relax. Brie, I promise I won't hurt you," he whispered softly.

As my body began to relax, his index finger christened my tight pucker. Never had I allowed anything to penetrate this sacred place, but with Cop it was different. He was the only man I trusted my body to. I was his. The pressure began to build in me as I felt the sense of fullness. With his cock inside me and his finger pushing deeper, I was on the verge of losing it. I could no longer hold on, my climax reached its capacity as my body shuddered with an earth-shattering orgasm.

Pulling my hair away from my sweat-covered face, Cope leaned over me and confessed. "I love you more than life itself. Please say you will be mine forever."

"Yours forever, Cop," I whispered. "I will love you for eternity."

CHAPTER TWENTY-FIVE

Cop

Spending this last couple of days with Brie had been beyond believable. I was glad when Lilly let her take the time off she needed in order to care for me. She was quite the little nurse maid. The only thing that was missing was the little white nurse's uniform that we could have a lot of fun with. I was also beginning to feel human again. Even though my side was still a little tender, it didn't stop me from getting what I needed, and the only thing I needed was to be making love to Brie

24/7, if I had my choice.

While Brie was at the market to get some much-needed groceries, I decide to try a few bouts with the punching bag. This was the best way that I knew of to get back on my feet. I was already feeling separation anxiety without Brie being around. Slipping on my boxing gloves, I tried to focus on the bag in front of me instead of the women I loved more and more each second. Stopping mid-jab, it hit me what I was just thinking. *"This is the woman I plan on spending the rest of my life with. What the hell am I waiting for?"*

With a smile on my face, I knew what I wanted from that moment. Jabbing the bag, I could feel the slightest pull on my side. It wasn't bad, it just felt tight. I was really out of shape and it was going to take time to reach my full potential again. Feeling the burn, I figured it was best not to push too much. I didn't want to overdo it. Looking down at my side, I hated looking at the nasty scar the bullet left. As ugly as it was, it was a constant reminder that I survived to be with the woman I loved. Pulling off my gloves, it was then that I knew what I needed to do.

Walking up the steps to the main floor, I grabbed my phone from the granite counter top and dialed Peter. "Peter, I needed a favor. Can you be at the cabin in twenty minutes?"

"Sure, what's up, bro?" he asked.

"I'll tell you when you get here."

~****~

I had never seen so many engagement rings in my life. It was like purchasing a new car. There were princess cuts, marquise, Asscher, emerald, radiant, the list went on and on. This was all new to me. But when the jeweler began talking about carats, clarity, and color, I began scratching my head. The only thing I was thankful for was that Peter was with me. He had been through this before. When the jeweler presented a princess-cut diamond with baguettes down the sides, I knew this would be the ring for Brie. It was beautiful. It didn't even matter that the cost was $12,000. She was worth every cent.

As we drove home, I could tell there was something on Peter's mind, the way his eyes kept shifting towards me. "Say what you need to say, Peter. You've been glaring at me since we left the jeweler," I said, perturbed.

"Okay, so here's the thing. I know that you really love Brie and she is a great girl, but don't you think you might be moving a little fast with this whole engagement thing?" he said.

"You know what, you're right. You know me better than anyone, but I'm telling you that after what happened to me, to her, I can't risk losing her. I think about her all the time, bro. I can't even think about her and not get a hard-on. I love her, man," I vowed.

"I understand, bro, you don't have to convince me. I just want to make sure this is what you really want."

"Damn straight it is," I confirmed. "I have not ever wanted anything more in my life."

Now that we got that out of the way, there was only one other question I had to ask. "So now that you know how I feel, how about you be my best man. That is, if she accepts."

"I'd be honored, bro," Peter said, reaching over to shake my hand.

When we pulled up to the cabin, Brie was unloading the groceries with the help of Ash. There was no way I was going to let her go anywhere without one of the guys going with her. As long as I was healing, that is. With Sean 'Scumbag' Bishop still out there, I wasn't about to take any chances that he would get to her.

Walking up to where she was standing, I took the three grocery bags she was holding. Damn, she was beautiful with her hair in messy piggy tails, and God, those shorts she wore should have been illegal. I could tell that Ash was thinking the same thing as his eyes wandered in the direction of her exceptional ass as she reached across the seat to grab another bag. When I gave him one of my trademark 'fuck off' looks, he lowered his head and proceeded to the cabin. It didn't matter what she wore, I knew that men were going to be gawking at her with hard-ons.

Setting the grub on the counter, Ash nodded with a thumbs-up letting me know he and Peter were out of there. Giving them an appreciative look, I said, "Thanks for the help, guys. Shop tomorrow, eight sharp." I wasn't asking, I was telling them I would be there ready to get back to work.

Turning my attention back to Brie, I said, "Babe let me put this away and cook something special for us. You go on up and take a nice bath. I'll let you know when dinner is ready." There was no argument from her as she kissed me on the cheek and headed up the stairs.

~****~

An hour and a half later, dinner was done, the table was set with tableware and lit candles. Tonight was as good a time as any to let Brie know how I really felt about her. As I finished up, I wondered what could be taking my baby so long. Pulling our dinner out of the oven and placing it on top to cool a bit, I decide to go check on my beautiful Brie. Walking up the stairs two at a time, I walked to the bedroom. The door was already partly open, which didn't surprise me; it was what was inside that got me. Sean was sitting on a chair in the corner, while Brie was on the bed with her arms behind her.

"What the fuck?" I cursed.

"It's about time you joined us," Sean said with a psychotic grin. "On your knees, you worthless piece of shit."

With the gun pointed straight at me, I had no other choice but to do what he asked. Getting to my knees, I lifted my hands in surrender. If there was a way that I could have ripped that fucking gun from his grasp without endangering Brie, I would have. "What do you want, Sean?"

"Let's see, where should I begin?" he began, as he snapped the cuffs around my wrists. "How about I kill you first and then take Ms. Sexy Pants away from here, someplace where no one will find us. Not even your tribe of alpha-male cronies."

"It doesn't matter where you take her. We will find her," I hissed as his foot landed on my side.

"What's the matter, Copper, did I hit your little setback? Didn't think I knew about that? Oh my, looks like the big guy's boo-boo is beginning to bleed. Maybe you'll just bleed to death and I won't have to waste a bullet on you," he sneered.

"You're a dead man, motherfucker," I cursed.

There was nothing I could do as his foot landed once again on my bad side. The pain was almost too much to handle, but I knew I needed to be strong and not let him see any weakness if I was going to get us out of this. I didn't have to put on a show too long. Looking up, I could see Peter and Ash walking across the driveway and towards the back door. I had never been so happy to see two guys in my life.

Sean got up from his seat and walked over to where Sabrina was. I had no idea what he was up to, but the guys needed to get here fast. Looking back at me with his shit-face grin he said, "You know what's worse than dying? Watching the girl you love getting fucked by someone else."

"What the fuck are you talking about, Bishop?" I cursed.

"I know you've been fucking my girl." He began turning his gaze back to Sabrina, rubbing the back of his hand along her cheek. "It's okay, sweetheart. I forgive you. Eye for an eye, right, Copper?"

I had no idea what he was talking about, but

when he lifted Sabrina from the bed and pulled down her shorts, I knew exactly what he had planned. "Leave her alone, you sick motherfucker."

"Just taking back what is mine," he chuckled.

"Sean, please don't do this," Sabrina cried.

It didn't matter how much she pleaded with him. He had his mouth on hers before she could finish. All I saw was red. There was no way he was going to lay another hand on her. I knew I needed to do something. The guys were taking too long to get here. With all my might, I rolled over and pushed to my feet. I plowed into Sean head first, causing him to drop the gun. I didn't even think about the possibility of it going off. I just wanted him off of Brie. Stumbling backwards, I somehow managed to get my cuffed arms under my legs so I could wrap my hands around his scrawny little neck. He was too quick. Before I could get to him, he had his hand on the gun, pointing it straight at Sabrina's head.

"Stupid, stupid, stupid. You really shouldn't have

done that. Not only do you get to watch me fuck her, you also get to watch me kill her," Sean hissed.

"Not going to happen, motherfucker," Peter's voice rang behind me.

Just as Sean diverted his attention to the door and moved the aim of his gun on Peter, within a split second he was on the floor. The bullet Peter fired landed on his neck, leaving him gurgling blood from his mouth. Before he took his last breath, he looked over to Sabrina and whispered, "I really did love you, Brie."

Ash was by my side getting the cuffs off my wrists. The minute they were off, I ran to Brie and held her in my arms. Grabbing the corner of the comforter, I pulled it over and covered her as much as I could. Her body was shaking so badly, I thought for sure she was having another attack. Placing my hand on her face, I tried to switch her focus from Sean to me. When her head moved in my direction, her tears began to fall. All I could think to do was hold her as tightly as possible. "It's okay, Brie. He will never hurt you again."

Ash was looking over Sean's body as I continued to comfort Brie. Crouching beside him, he turned Sean's head and placed his hand over his eyes, pulling Sean's eyes closed. All I could think about was Brie. She had been through so much the past couple of weeks. I really needed to take her away from here, someplace where we didn't have to deal with this crap for a while.

CHAPTER TWENTY-SIX
Sabrina

"Sabrina, baby, we have to go. If we don't leave right now we are going to miss our flight," I heard Cop yelling at me as he rolled our suitcases to the front door.

"I am trying to hurry. I just need to make sure I didn't forget anything!" I said frantically.

"Well, it feels like you've got everything you need in this suitcase. Jesus, babe, this thing weights a ton."

Looking over the stair railing, I watched as Cop lifted my overstuffed suitcase out the door. I couldn't help but smile at the way his muscles flexed as he lifted the bag off the floor. After everything that had happened to us, he wanted to take me away. I was perfectly okay with staying here and locking ourselves in the bedroom for two weeks.

Everything about what happened to Sean and Lee and what they did finally came out. Turns out after we split, Sean was already putting a plan in place on how he was going to get me back. He bought the old missile site through some auction the state had and turned it into his home. The money that he made selling drugs and weapons was supposed to go back to Lee, with him only getting a small cut. When Lee found out that Sean ripped him off, he began his revenge. He only learned about me through Sean's continued efforts to get me back while we were in college. Somehow Lee found out about my mom and her being in prison. When he went to visit her, he had to tie up loose ends, especially knowing that my real father was the man he killed years ago for double crossing him, so he had someone inside the correctional facility kill her. I wasn't even heartbroken when Cop told me. I think it was a relief more than anything that she finally got what I couldn't do.

Finding me was Lee's only plan. He needed to convince me that I was his daughter in hopes that I would trust him enough to tell him where Sean was. The problem with that plan was that I had no idea, nor did I care. The sad thing about it was that I almost believed him. I'm glad he got what he deserved. Maybe someone inside would make him their girlfriend.

Taking a second look around to make sure I hadn't left anything, I headed downstairs where Cop was patiently waiting for me. He looked so alpha-male with his arms crossed at his chest and his ankle resting over the other. Very macho. Jogging down the steps, I pushed to my toes and said, "Let's go, big guy," before I planted a small peck on his lips.

I could feel the smile begin to creep up on his face as he took my hand and spun me around so that my back was to his chest. The feeling of his breath on my neck had me all undone. I knew if we didn't get out of there, we were going to miss our flight. I was trying to escape, but Cop had me in his arms with his soft lips planted on mine. There was no way that I could protest, nor did I have the will to stop. I would never deny Cop a kiss, especially since his mouth felt good on mine. So good that the heat was already beginning to build between my legs. Wrapping my arms around his shoulders, Cop lifted me from the floor and had my back against the wall in a split second. I always wondered how he could do that maneuver so quickly. It had something to do with his self-defense experience, I was pretty sure.

Cop began expertly removing my clothes one piece at a time. While he was removing mine, I was having no luck with his. With the majority of my clothes off, everything except my bra, Cop switched gears and began taking his own clothes off while still pressing my body snugly to the wall. I couldn't believe the amount of strength this man had. It was effortless for him to hold me in place with one hand while he removed his clothes with the other. Pushing his jeans down his legs, he lowered them just enough that he was able to step out of them.

It took him little time before I felt the tip of his glorious cock push between my folds. He knew my body so well and knew just the spot he needed to touch in order for it to send me over the edge. Pumping in and out of me, I heard him moan, "This is going to be quick and fast, baby"

Taking him the best I could in that position, I slid a hand between our bodies and began stimulating my clit by making small circles around the swollen nub. I could feel the onset of my release as Cop pushed deeper and deeper inside me. Between the friction of his dick moving inside me and the tender slow pleasure I was giving my clit, my body could no longer hold on. I needed this, I needed to come. It was only after I heard the words, "You are so fucking tight, Brie," that my release took over and my creaming liquid covered him with a white blanket.

Cop must have been close as well because with no warning, he screamed, "God, fucking shit," before his seed spilled inside me.

There was a small smile on my face, showing how much I loved making him come.

~****~

Cop took care of everything at the ticketing booth when we got to the airport. I had never been to Hawaii, but have always wanted to go. I knew that it was going to be an eleven-hour flight. I was so glad that Cop had purchased first-class tickets for our flight. I couldn't even begin to imagine sitting for that long in a coach seat with no room to even stretch. Getting to our gate, the first-class passengers were already beginning to board. Cop handed the attendant our tickets and we proceeded down the gangway to the plane. This was going to be the best trip for us. Just the two of us. No more drama, only great food, sunny beaches, and relaxation.

Finding our seats, Cop put our carry-on bag in the overhead compartment. Both of our gazes fell upon the couple sitting across from us as their lips were latched together in a heated kiss. I wondered if they ever heard of the Mile High Club and if they would be taking their affection further. Looking at me with those gorgeous brown eyes, he leaned over and whispered, "When in Rome."

His lips were on mine in an instant. I forgot where we were as I pulled him closer to me to get more of those lips I loved so much. It was only after the flight attendant cleared her voice, that I realized we were creating a little show for the rest of the passengers. Looking down on us, she said with a smile, "Buckle up, we are about to take off."

This was the biggest, most embarrassing moment of all time. I knew my cheeks were as red as the scarf she was wearing around her neck. Lowering my head, I tried to hide my shame. I could hear Cop laughing beside me. I wasn't sure why he was laughing considering half the embarrassment should have been his.

We ended up having to change planes at LAX, which was fine with me. It gave us about an hour to get to our next gate, stretch our feet, and grab something quick to eat. When it was time for us to board again, my stomach was happy, and I had worked out all the kinks from flying. As we boarded the plane, the same couple was seated right beside us. They looked so in love as he helped her with her luggage and held her as they sat. It was so romantic.

I think the flight from California to Hawaii flew by in an instant. When the pilot announced the final descent, I could have jumped for joy. Soon we would be landing on the beautiful island of Honolulu.

The minute the door open and we were allowed to exit, we both jumped up, grabbed our things, and made our way to baggage claim. Getting out of the airport was a snap. After we picked up our luggage, we headed outside where we would be able to hail a cab. The drive to the hotel was beautiful. I had never seen so many gorgeous flowers in my life. As the driver kept driving, Cop pulled me in closer and whispered so the driver couldn't hear his thoughts. "When we get to our room at the hotel, all of these things are coming off."

I had to giggle at his confession. There was nothing more that I wanted than to have those strong arms around me. His eyes fell upon mine and I could feel the love he had for me. Before our lips met he said in a commanding voice, "Step on it and there's an extra fifty in it for you,"

I never knew how sexy he really was until he pulled my body onto his lap and planted his mouth on mine. We went at each other like a couple of love-struck teenagers. I could only imagine what the driver must have thought about our PDA. I was so glad went the driver pulled up to our hotel. Now we could really begin our vacation; that was, if we actually left the room during our two-week stay.

~****~

It was early afternoon and I was exhausted. The eleven-hour flight got the best of me. Cop volunteered to empty the suitcases while I took a shower and then a short nap. The hotel was putting on a huge luau tonight on the beach and we didn't want to miss it. Stripping off my clothing, I turned the nozzle on in the shower and waited for it to heat up. Looking in the mirror, I could see a pair of tired but happy eyes staring at me. As I stepped into the shower, I let the warm water consume me. Every ache in my body was diminished by the pulsating power of the shower head. As I was absorbing the relaxing spray, the shower door opened and Cop was there, standing naked in all his gorgeousness. Placing his hand on my waist, I could feel the touch of his hands as they caressed my body. I could feel his breath on the back of my neck and down my shoulder as a blazing inferno began to consume my body with each kiss he placed on my skin. His soft breath turned into a whisper as he said, "Place your hands on the wall, baby, and don't move them."

Doing as he commanded, I pressed my hands against the cool tile and seized every touch, every kiss he showered me with. Cop lowered his hand between the valley of my ass cheeks, sending a tingle between my legs. The last time he had entered me from behind, I had loved it and my orgasm had sprung like a waterfall raining down in a tropical forest. Drawing me away from my thoughts, a slight slap landed on my butt cheek as Cop moaned, "Spread your legs wider so I can consume that sweet pussy."

Spreading my legs, I could feel his body dip as his hands ran down the length of my legs. His mouth pressed against my ass and I could feel the tiny nips of his teeth as he sucked and kissed me. The tight squeeze of my cheeks between his fingers sent me reeling as he continued the assault with his mouth gliding his tongue between my cheeks to the apex of my sex. When his tongue dipped inside my channel, the feeling was so good, it took everything I had not to come. Reaching around me, he placed his hand over my mound with his index finger doing magic on my clit. As wonderful as this felt, I wanted more. With a heated rush, I pleaded breathlessly, "Cop, I need to feel you inside me."

Wasting no time, Cop got to his feet, spun me around and had his lips on mine. The taste of my juices on his tongue sent my body soaring. Lifting my leg and wrapping them around his slim waist, his impressive cock stilled at the gate of my entrance before he gently pushed inside. My walls began to stretch taking him in inch by blissful inch. Unable to get enough, needing more of him, I moaned, "Cop, I need you deeper inside me."

Cop lifted my body from the tile floor and I wrapped my other leg around him as he pushed my heat-driven body against the tile wall, cooling the fever within. His movements increased, filling my body with a surge unlike anything I have ever felt before. Thrust after thrust, he pushed deeper inside me. Capturing the one spot to send me over the edge, Cop stilled for a moment so that I could feel the pulsation of his cock inside. He knew just what I needed. Continuing his efforts, my body opened and my release took over. I was his.

CHAPTER TWENTY-SEVEN
Sabrina

After finishing my explosive shower with Cop, I decided to take a nap while he went to check out the rest of the hotel. He thought it would be nice to get some information about the island so he could plan the rest of our trip. I couldn't wait to see what he decided on. I was sure whatever it was, it would be amazing. Closing my eyes, it wasn't long until my mind began to wander. I kept thinking about what my life would have been like if I hadn't met Cop. I also started to think about how much

I wanted to spend the rest of my life with this man. I knew that he loved me, but didn't know how he felt about being with me forever.

My thoughts must have gotten the best of me, because I was no longer tired. Pushing from the bed, I decided to spend a few moments on the balcony and take in some of the fresh Hawaiian air. Opening the sliding glass door, the warm breeze blew the sheer drapes open and I stepped outside. We had a perfect view of the ocean from where the room was. The hotel was also within walking distance from the beach. As I looked over the edge, I could see dozens of people laying out by the pool soaking in the sun. There was even some sort of water volleyball game going on in the pool.

Turning on my heels, I grabbed my shades and cell, and put on my flip-flops and headed down. On the way down, I called Cop to let him know that I couldn't sleep after all and would be waiting for him at the pool. When he didn't answer, I decided to leave him a text message. Walking out into the open area leading to the pool, I could smell the scent of coconut oil laced with the smell of blossoms. There was a bar nestled in a shaded area that look pretty busy, but the drinks that were lined up on top looked amazing and I could use a little refreshment. As I sat on one of the bar stools. I watched as the bartender began making me a drink called the 'Tropical Paradise.' As he placed a little green umbrella in the fruity concoction and slid it front of me, I could feel the touch of a strong hand on my shoulder.

"I'll have one of those as well," Cop requested, taking a seat beside me.

Turning towards him, I placed my legs between his and leaned over. The minute our eyes met, his lips were on mine. The fruity coolness of his tongue filled my senses as I tasted the mixture of pineapple, banana, and coconut on his lips. "Mmm, you taste good," I confessed between breaths.

"Let's finish these. I have a great day planned," Cop said.

~****~

Cop was right, he did have a day filled with adventure planned for us. The first thing we did was take a drive up to the Manoa Falls. It was breathtaking. Once we got to the top, the hike was well worth it. The waterfall was amazing. I could have stared at it for hours. Heading back down the trail, we knew that it was getting late and it was a thirty-minute drive to the hotel. The luau that the hotel was doing was only a couple of hours away, and this was one thing I didn't want to miss.

Even though this was our first day on the island, our trip so far was amazing. Tomorrow Cop had planned for us to go for a little boat ride and then take in some of the other sights. At first he wanted to take me snorkeling, but since I didn't know how to swim, he found something comparable to do. When we got back to the States, I needed to make sure to take some swimming lessons. There was so much I was missing out on by not knowing how to swim.

Getting back to the hotel room in record time, we decide to take a quick shower together, only it didn't end up being quick at all. The exploration of each other's body took over. I loved every inch of Cop's body, just like he loved mine. It didn't matter that we were both sporting a nasty scar. His was on his left side and mine was on the right. When we were finished being thoroughly fucked, we stepped out of the shower and dried off. Cop allowed me to have the bathroom first since it would take me longer to get ready, only it was hard to get ready with him sitting on the commode staring up at me with those gorgeous brown eyes.

"How am I supposed to get ready when you are looking at me like that?" I questioned.

"You're so beautiful, baby, I could stare at you for hours," he confessed.

"We don't have hours, Cop. I needed to get ready." I watched him stand and walk towards me. With a soft touch to my cheek, he bent down and kissed me tenderly on the forehead and walked away.

~****~

Even thought we were only fifteen minutes late, the luau was already in full swing. The Tiki torches were already lit and several people were already seated on the low tables that were lining the stage area where the dancers would be performing. I had read about the entertainment in the hotel brochure, but never imagined it would be this exciting. Taking our place, we were greeted with a pair of flowered leis. As the young Hawaiian girl placed them over our heads, the scent of Plumeria filled the air.

The music began a short time later with the beat of drums. Soon about a dozen men appeared carrying lit torches and wearing very little clothing. The atmosphere was filled with music and dancing as more performers came on the stage. There were even hula girls of all ages doing the traditional dance. Some of the guests were even pulled from their tables to join in on the festivities. My eyes were fixed on the flame dancers when a gentleman came up to Cop and whispered something in his ear. I could only wonder what was said, as I watched Cop nodded his head in agreement.

It was only after Cop pushed his chair from the table and stood that I knew something was up. Holding out his hand, he took mine and said softly, "Come with me, baby. There is something I need to show you."

I wasn't sure what was going on, but I took his cue and placed my cloth napkin on the table and followed him down a grassy path leading to the beach.

As soon as the white sand appeared, he took a left turn and my heart began to beat faster than it had ever before. There before me was a white canopy covering a table set for two with candles on top and lit torches leading a path to the beautiful set up. Looking over at him, I could see the love in his eyes as my eyes began to fill with tears. Pulling me near, he kissed me gently on the temple while whispering softly. "I love you, Brie."

"I love you too, Cop," I said, taking in his touch.

Cop: Jagged Edge Series #2

As we sat down at the perfectly displayed table, a row of servers came down the path carrying what I suspected were traditional dishes of the island. After assisting us with the most amazing meal I had ever seen, the servers left in the same order that they had arrived. Taking in the aroma of the various foods in front of us, we began to feast on this wonderful meal. The flavor of everything made my taste buds very happy.

Completely stuffed, I placed my silverware across my plate, and took a sip of wine to wash the last of this magnificent meal down. Placing my glass on the table, I watched as Cop stood from his seat. The look in his eyes was more breathtaking than the surroundings he had arranged for me. Walking over to me, he took my hands and placed them in his. Getting down on one knee, my heart began to sink.

"Brie, I know that we have only known each other for a short time, but I feel like I have known you for a lifetime. You have been the one woman that I have been searching my whole life for. Your kindness, and tenderness have drawn me in. Your beauty has captivated me. Your strength has amazed me. You have truly captured my heart. I love you from the bottom of my heart. I want to spend the rest of my life with you, Sabrina Roberts. Please say that you want that too, and marry me."

The love I had for this man made my heart bleed. Not in the broken irreparable way, but in such a way that if anything would ever happen to Cop, I would simply die. So I answered him with a definite, "Yes, I'll marry you. A thousand times over."

Cop pulled a tiny white box from his pocket and flipped open the top. When the ring can into view, my heart sang to see how unbelievably beautiful it was. As he slipped the princess-cut diamond that had to be at least two carats on my finger, the tears that I had been holding back came showering down.

"I hope those are tears of happiness and not because you hate the ring," Cop said.

"They are. Every one of them. The ring is

beautiful, Cop. I love you."

CHAPTER TWENTY-EIGHT
Sabrina

This by far was the best evening I had ever had. After we had finished our meal on the beach, we took a long walk, Cop admiring me, while I admired my ring. The night was beautiful. The sky was so clear, allowing the stars to reflect on the blue water. As we walked hand in hand, Cop turned to me and said, "Let's go back to the room."

I didn't protest because that was exactly what I

was thinking. Walking back to the hotel, the Luau was still in full swing. Even though I had missed most of the entertainment, I wouldn't have changed anything about this evening. It was perfect.

Reaching our room, Cop slid the key card in the slot and turned the handle. The minute the door closed, he had my body pressed to the wall with his lips pressed to mine. Pulling him closer, I wanted more of him. As the kiss deepened my heart began to race as the electricity took over. Cop's hand glided lower down my body until they rested on my ass. Caressing it lightly, he lifted me from the floor and walked us towards the bedroom. It was all I could do to contain my desire for this man.

Setting me down, he slowly began removing my clothes, kissing every inch of my body as more of my naked skin was revealed. Completely naked before him with the wetness pooling between my legs, I watched as he began shedding his own clothes. With his body completely bare and on display for me to consume, Cop walked over to where I was standing speechless, just taking in his body while he carried me over to the side of the bed. Setting me down gently, he leaned over and gave me a soft kiss on my lips, then my forehead before asking with a soft whisper, "Do you trust me, baby?"

Looking up at him, trying to figure out what he was planning, I said with pure honesty, "I trust you with everything, Cop."

"Good," he replied as he pushed from the bed and headed to the bathroom.

As I sat and waited for his return, I patiently held back my desire for him. When he returned with two sashes that he had taken from the robes hanging on the bathroom door, my mind began reeling as to what he was going to do. Sitting beside me, he said in a low commanding tone, "Give me your hands, Brie."

Holding them out in front of me, I watched as he began tying the silky material around my wrists. Once they were secure, he stood and took hold of my ankles, pulling my body down the bed so that I was now lying down. With my hands resting on my stomach, Cop gently lifted them above my head and expertly secured them to the bamboo headboard.

Taking hold of the remaining sash, he placed it over my eyes blindfolding me. Even being in his complete control, I felt relaxed and safe. I knew that I could trust him. Pulling me from my thoughts, he bent over and kissed me on the lips. In between breaths, he said, "If it gets to be too much, you know what to say."

Nodding my head, I waited for his next move. His hands began caressing the bare skin on my stomach. Since I could only feel, I knew he was tracing the faint scar that I had received so many years ago. I could feel the softness of his lips on my stomach as he began trailing kisses along the line of my scar. "You are so beautiful, baby," he said, continuing to kiss me.

I wished I could touch him. He moved up my body, kissing every sensitized inch. When he got to my breast, the tingling feeling in my body heightened and my back lifted from the bed, willing him to give me more. There was a slight pinch and suck on my hard nipple, making the wetness pool between my legs. Everything he was doing was setting my body on fire. He knew exactly what I needed. His hand dipped lower, finding my slick folds. Spreading my legs wider, I could feel the separation of my folds as his finger began rubbing between them. His finger entered me and my body came undone. Each stroke sent me closer and closer to the place I never wanted to leave. As he lowered his body further down mine, I could feel his mouth at the juncture of my mound before it found its way to my swollen clit. With his tongue, Cop began swirling it slowly while another finger plunged inside me. Every nerve in my body was on stimulation overload. When I felt his fingers pull out only to be replaced by his tongue, all my inhibitions were lost as the gate holding back my release opened and his name spilled from my lips.

As his mouth came up to mine in a deep kiss. I could taste the remnants of my own juices on his lips. It was the sexiest thing I had ever done. With his body pressed to mine, he slowly began moving his hips as his cock entered my wet channel. Wrapping my legs around his waist, was all I could do to pull him in closer. His movements began to increase and I felt my walls tighten around him. Each thrust of his cock pushed deeper and deeper as I continued to suck him in. When his movements stopped and the pulsation inside me began, I knew that he was close. With one last thrust, his explosion erupted like a tidal wave. It was only after he called out my name that I knew there would never be another man for me.

When his release subsided, Cop removed my blindfold and looked into my eyes. "Baby, are you okay?"

As my eyes focused on him through tears of happiness, I said softly, "I love you so much, Cop."

"I love you too, baby," he replied, moving a stray hair from my face.

With my hands still tied to the bed and this gorgeous man on top of me, I only had one thing on my mind. With a mischievous grin, I looked to him and said, "Can we do that again?"

The smile on his face said it all as he placed the blindfold over my eyes and once again worshiped me.

About the Author

My passion for writing began a little over two years ago when I retired from a nine to five job. Even though I enjoyed working, I wanted something different. It was then that I decided that I wanted to write. Romance and passion is a topic that everyone desires in life, and it is for that reason I decided to write Erotic romances. Finding my niche as a romance writer has not only filled my heart, but also has kept me young. When I'm not writing, I like to spend time outside taking long walks and sipping wine under the stars.

I hope you found **Cop** enjoyable to read. Please consider taking the time to share your thoughts and leave a review on the on-line bookstore. It would make the difference in helping another reader decide to read this and my upcoming collection in the Jagged Edge Series.

To get up–to-date information on when the next Jagged Edge Series will be released click on the following link http://allong6.wix.com/allongbooks and add your information to my mailing list. There is also something extra for you when you join.

Also By A. L. Long

Shattered Innocence

Next to Never: Shattered Innocence Trilogy

Next to Always (Book Two): Shattered Innocence Trilogy

Next to Forever (Book Three): Shattered Innocence Trilogy

Jagged Edge Series

Hewitt: Jagged Edge Series #1

Cop: Jagged Edge Series #2

Coming Soon!!!!!!

Jagged Edge Series

Hawk: Jagged Edge Series #3

To keep up with all the latest releases:

Twitter:

http://twitter.com/allong1963

Facebook:

http://www.facebook.com/ALLongbooks

Official Website:

http://www.allongbooks.com